STATE FAIR

A BUR OAK BOOK

STATE FAIR

BY

PHIL STONG

UNIVERSITY OF IOWA PRESS ⨂ IOWA CITY

University of Iowa Press, Iowa City 52242

Copyright © 1932 by the Century Company,

copyright © 1959 by Virginia Swain Stong

Foreword copyright © 1996 by the University of Iowa Press

www.uiowapress.org

Printed in the United States of America

ISBN 978-0-87745-569-1

Library of Congress Catalog Card Number 96-60644

This edition is reprinted courtesy of the Harold Matson Company, Inc., 276 Fifth Avenue, New York NY 10001.

Cover design by Kristina Kachele, llc

Printed on acid-free paper

Drawing on page iii by Ed Lindlof

CONTENTS

Robert A. McCown

THE ENJOYMENT of a good book is sometimes enhanced by a brief immersion into the historical background of the work and a condensed look at the facts and events in the life of the writer.

The author of *State Fair*, Philip Duffield Stong, was born on January 27, 1899, near Pittsburg, Iowa, a village no longer found on maps. Pittsburg was on the west side of the Des Moines River in southeast Iowa's Van Buren County. Young Phil was the son of Benjamin and Ada Evesta Duffield Stong. Father Ben ran a general store in Pittsburg and then later a variety store in Keosauqua, the county seat of Van Buren County, where he was also postmaster.

Phil Stong went to grade and high school in Keosauqua and then to Drake University in Des Moines, Iowa's capital. At Drake he majored in English, minored in German, and wrote a senior thesis on the aesthetics of Schiller and Santayana. After graduation in 1919 he taught in the high school at Biwabik, Minnesota, a town on the Mesabi Iron Range north of Duluth. During that 1919–1920 school year he gave instruction in physical training and manual training as well as coaching football and basketball. The young man found life in Biwabik fascinating because of the many different ethnic groups in the town. Later, Stong set a novel (*The Iron Mountain*) and a children's book (*Honk: The Moose*) in the Iron Range. After a year in Minnesota's far north, he went to New York City for graduate work in English at Columbia University. The years 1921 to 1923 found him in Neodesha, Kansas, where he taught English, coached the debate team, and managed school publications. While spending two and a half years in southeastern Kansas, Stong took correspondence courses in education from the University of Kansas. Then, in 1924, Stong returned to Des Moines to teach journalism at Drake and coach debate.[1]

Turning from teaching to the practice of journalism, Phil Stong went to work as a reporter and editorial writer for the *Des Moines Register*. During all of this time, he was striving to become a creative writer. As early as November 1921 he had a story in *The Midland*, an important regional literary magazine edited by John T. Frederick.[2] In 1925, at age twenty-six, Stong returned to New York, where he worked first as a wire editor for the

Foreword

Associated Press and then as a copy editor and feature writer for the North American Newspaper Alliance. In 1927 he went to Boston to interview Nicola Sacco and Bartolomeo Vanzetti just before their execution, an experience he considered one of the most important in his life.[3] Later, he was with the magazines *Liberty* and *Editor and Publisher*, Sunday feature editor of the newspaper the *New York World*, and finally an advertising writer for Young and Rubicam.

On November 8, 1925, at the time he moved to New York, Phil Stong married Virginia Maude Swain, who was also a newspaper reporter. Stong credited her with encouraging him in his writing. The year before his death, Stong reminisced about the beginnings of his most famous novel: "I was working in the publicity department of one of the few good advertising firms in the world when Mrs. Stong suggested that I do something about my native State's great harvest festival, the Fair."[4] This happened in the summer of 1931. On July 28, he wrote to the "Folks" back in Iowa: "I've finally got a novel coming in fine shape. I've done 10,000 words on it in three days and I get more enthusiastic every day. . . . I hope I can hold up this time. I always write 10,000 swell words and then go to pieces."[5]

State fairs were a subject that Phil Stong knew well.

Foreword

For several years his grandfather had been superinten-
dent of the swine division at the Iowa State Fair. Then,
while a reporter with the *Des Moines Register*, Stong was
assigned to cover the evening stock shows at the fair.
American agricultural fairs were and still are a combina-
tion of education and festivity: exhibitions, demonstrations,
competition for premiums, horse racing, grandstand entertainment, and carnival attractions. Iowa held its first state
fair in 1854, and for some time fairs were held at various
locations around the state before permanently settling in
Des Moines. As years went by, the fairs drew larger
crowds and became more elaborate. Judging of livestock,
for instance, became more scientific when professors
from Iowa State University took over from amateur com-
mittees. For rural folks, the fair was a wonderful opportunity to get away from home, see old friends, and meet
new people. Many families camped at the fair as they
had done at tent Chautauquas in small towns.

The plot of *State Fair* is simple. Each member of the
Frake family attends the fair with a purpose: Father Abel
Frake, farmer and stockbreeder, wants his Hampshire
boar "Blue Boy" to win the sweepstakes. Abel's wife,
Melissa, wants to win blue ribbons for her pickles. Son
Wayne wants revenge at the hoop-la stand, a carnival
game in which prizes are won by tossing rings. And

daughter Margy wants some fun. Wayne and Margy are also looking for romantic adventures. "The Frakes had stepped for a moment into a fantasy."[6]

State Fair is very much an Iowa book, filled with incidents and details from the author's own life. While the setting of a state fair in the early part of the twentieth century is accurately portrayed, Stong was of course writing as a novelist and not as a historian. There is undeniably an element of make-believe in *State Fair*. The author was creating an artistic representation of the fair, not presenting the literal truth. As always, Stong was bubbling with whimsy and humor.

The novel appeared in the late spring of 1932 and was widely reviewed.[7] While most of the notices were favorable, Iowans tended to think that the Frake children were "loose." In a letter to his college roommate, Stong wrote: "Iowa generally felt that Iowa girls wouldn't do such things."[8] At the end of the year a good review in England prompted this comment: ". . . and even the wounds left in my hide by the Tama Tribune and the What Cheer Gazette are beginning to heal over nicely."[9] Another pleasant emollient was money. After publication by the Century Company, the book became a Literary Guild Selection and was reprinted in 1933 by Grosset and Dunlap. Subsequently, there were foreign editions, paperbacks, and even an Armed Services edition. In the fall of 1932, Hollywood made a film of the book with Will Rogers starring as Abel Frake. In 1945 the book became a musical motion picture with Vivian Blaine and Jeanne Crain and some memorable songs by Rodgers and Hammerstein, such as "Grand Night for Singing" and "It Might as Well be Spring." A film with a Texas setting was released in 1962 and, in the spring of 1996, a Broadway show was adapted from the Hammerstein screenplay. With the income he earned from *State Fair*, Stong was able to buy his mother's family farm, the George C. Duffield Estate called "Linwood Farm," just north of the ghost town of Pittsburg on the west side of the Des Moines River. The author made many improvements on the farm, which he then rented to a tenant.

After his success with *State Fair*, Phil Stong went on to write more than forty books, many of them set in the Keosauqua area. When not writing adult fiction, he tried his hand at children's books. "I use the pieces to clear my throat between books to remind myself that direction, simplicity, and suspense are the *sine qua non* of all narrative writing."[10] His favorite among his own books was *Buckskin Breeches* (1937), a historical novel based on his grandfather Duffield's memories of frontier Iowa.[11]

Foreword

Phil Stong died at his home in rural western Connecticut in 1957, but his most famous book lives on in this new edition.

NOTES

1. The basic facts of Phil Stong's life can be found in Clarence A. Andrews, "Stong, Phil(lip Duffield)," in *Dictionary of American Biography*, Supplement Six, 1956–1960, 603–604. See also Phil Stong, *If School Keeps* (New York: Stokes, 1940), an unusual autobiography which recounts Stong's schooling, his career as a teacher, and his opinions on education.

2. Phil Stong, "Hymeneal," *The Midland*, 7 (November 1921), 370–385.

3. Phil Stong, "The Last Days of Sacco and Vanzetti," in *The Aspirin Age*, 1919–1941, ed. by Isabel Leighton (New York: Simon and Schuster, 1949), 169–189, and Fred Somkin, "How Vanzetti Said Goodbye," *Journal of American History*, 68 (September 1981), 298–312.

4. Letter, Phil Stong to Cyril Clemens, February 23, 1956, Manuscript Letters Collection, Special Collections Department, University of Iowa Libraries, Iowa City.

5. Letter, Phil Stong to "Folks," July 28, 1931, Phil Stong Papers, Cowles Library, Drake University, Des Moines.

6. Phil Stong, *State Fair* (New York: Century Co., 1932), 252.

7. Among the major reviews were Louis Kronenberger, "The Brighter Side of Farm Life," *New York Times Book Review*, May 8, 1932, 6; Robert Cantwell, "This Side of Paradise," *New Republic*,

71 (July 6, 1932), 215–216; Garreta Busey, "Middle West New Style," *New York Herald Tribune Books*, May 8, 1932, 1–2; and Arthur Ruhl, "Iowa, Old Style," *Saturday Review of Literature*, 8 (May 7, 1932), 713.

8. Letter, Phil Stong to Harvey Davis, September 19, 1932, Manuscript Letters Collection, Special Collections Department, University of Iowa Libraries, Iowa City.

9. Letter, Phil Stong to "Folks," December 9, 1932, Stong Papers, Drake University.

10. "Phil Stong," in *More Junior Authors* (New York: H. W. Wilson, 1963), 197.

11. Louie W. Attebery, "Phil Stong's *Buckskin Breeches*," *Palimpsest*, 68 (Winter 1987), 184–188.

SATURDAY EVENING

STATE FAIR

CHAPTER I

SATURDAY EVENING

ABEL FRAKE solemnly appraised the cigar which the Storekeeper laid before him. It was a thing of beautiful curves and a rich brown coat; its wrapper was limp and silky, and though, for all his air of connoisseurship, Abel knew no more about a cigar than any other smoker in Brunswick, he felt instinctively that this was good. For, finally, it was not a nickel cigar, but a three-for-a-quarter cigar —practically a ten-cent cigar.

With a consenting gesture he signaled for two more. "It's not reasonable a man should burn up the price of eight eggs—ten good days' work for a fair hen—in a Saturday evening and Sunday," he said, "but a man shouldn't stint himself all the time—it's only once a week."

3

The Storekeeper, only a little more than middle-aged despite the gray at his temples and the bald spot running up his high forehead, noted the purchase on a paper sack, at the end of a long line of figures. "You'd buy three nickel cigars anyway, Abel; you're just out ten cents. Next week you just work each one of your hens a little harder and you'll have that dime made up in no time."

Abel laughed. "You ever try to push extra work out of a hen? A hen ain't the kind you can push. Anyway, I guess it wouldn't do me much good to drive 'em. Mama gets all the money from the hens for Fair Week and Christmas presents."

The Storekeeper smiled at Melissa Frake ironically. "You ever see any of that money, Mrs. Frake?"

Melissa's plump, agreeable face assumed a mock severity. "You can bet I do! I'm not saying it isn't a fight sometimes to keep it away from a man like Abel Frake, but I'm a match for him!"

The circle of loafers against the counters laughed softly with an effect almost choral. Years of laughing together at the proper moments had taught each of them to submerge his laughter in the group's. It was the unconscious response of men of uncertain social instincts.

"You sure you've got everything?" the Storekeeper asked.

Mrs. Frake slipped into a mild trance, checking off items in the air with her finger. While this thaumaturgy progressed, the loafers were respectfully silent. "Everything," she said, at last.

The Storekeeper, fully conscious of what was to ensue, began to arrange the heap of packages so that they could be easily divided. Mrs. Frake took a few steps this way, a few steps that way, and stared about at the great roomful of goods. Thirty feet of shelves, stretching from floor to ceiling, carried dry goods. There were cases containing harmonicas, air-rifles, hair-pins, patent medicines, and school-books. At the back of the store was the tiny office with its safe, which said, "Please don't blow up this safe, it is just in case of fire. If you turn the knob it will open. Probably it will open if you just kick it."

Before the office was a rack of overalls, coats, and ready-made clothing. The Storekeeper stood behind a counter on the side of the store devoted to groceries and shoes. The hardware stock was in an adjoining room, unlighted. The main room was filled with the greenish-white glare of a gasoline-pressure lighting system.

"I think I might take a little sackful of candy," said Mrs. Frake. "Maybe a package of chewing-gum for after dinner to-morrow."

The Storekeeper took two doubtful steps, as if the proposition were much too dubitable to justify his actually going to the candy counter.

"There it is," said Abel Frake, with unconvincing bitterness, "just because you work me into a little bit of extravagance she thinks she has to throw away the whole family fortune."

"I'm just as much entitled to my candy as you are to your cigars, Abel Frake," said Melissa with an attempt at fierceness, pouting lips which were still red and firm. "I guess I will have some candy," she added defiantly, to the Storekeeper, for the five-hundred-and-twentieth time in ten years of fifty-two Saturdays each.

"Maybe she could make those hens work harder, Abel," said one of the loafers. "You say they're her hens." But this was said for only the one-hundred-and-fourth time, for it had been invented only two years before. Again the sympathetic moan of laughter filled the bright, shadowy room.

Abel uttered a low groan. "What kind of candy will it be, Mrs. Frake?" asked the Storekeeper, triumphantly, as though he had just accomplished a miracle of salesmanship.

Her eyes glowed over the assortment of cheap nougats, gum-drops, hard sugar candies with colored flowers on their ends, pasty candy bananas, chocolate creams of an early vintage. The Storekeeper waited as though a decision were being made—as though she would not finally take ten cents' worth of chocolate caramels "with just a few lemon-drops and a few pink peppermints—Margy likes them."

"I think," she said finally, "I'll take ten cents' worth of hard chocolates with just a few lemon-drops and a few pink peppermints—Margy likes them." The Storekeeper weighed out twelve cents' worth of candy.

"And a package of Bloodmint Gum." Hastily. It was the five-hundred-and-twentieth afterthought of the ten years.

"How's Blue Boy looking, Abel?" The Storekeeper looked up over his scales, which showed that he was about to make one fourth of a cent on a fifteen-cent transaction.

"Going to take him out of stud pretty soon. If he doesn't take sweepstakes at the Fair this year it's just about going to break up the whole Frake family—including Eph." Eph was the Hired Man. "Looks better than he looked last year—when he should've had it. They're going to have to raise some powerful hogs if they keep him out of the grand award this year."

The store door protested and opened and two women entered. There was a babel of "Why, Melissa!"—"Why, Martha!"—"Alice, did you get that hat over in Pittsville?" and the three ladies withdrew to the show window—which was full of sacks of chicken-feed—disposed themselves comfortably on the sacks and began to talk in low but animated voices.

The loafers, with the Storekeeper and Abel Frake, on the other hand moved to the darker portion of the store near the ready-made suits. It was the Brunswick equivalent of the ladies' retirement to the drawing-room. A mild but hearty spirit of

8

celebration filled the place. It was Saturday—eight thirty, the very height of the evening.

The Storekeeper dropped his professional manner—very superficial at best—without any perceptible effort. The experiences of twenty years of country storekeeping had lined the Storekeeper's face with amiable, ironic lines. He believed, with Jack London's Sea Wolf, that Heaven ordains all things for the worst—but more mischievously than tragically. He thought of God as a slightly perverse, omnipotent small child, breaking His jam jars all over the Storekeeper's life. He gathered up the pieces and shook his finger at God.

"There's just one thing you want to watch out for, Abel," he said seriously. "Don't let your hog get too good."

Abel grinned as he awaited the resolution of this statement, for all Brunswick knew that the Storekeeper was slightly and amusingly mad. They respected his madness, for when the World War started he had crammed his store with stock, explaining that it was beyond belief that our Senators and Representatives in Congress should show the slight intelligence necessary to keep us out of it, and that prices would be higher. As a result he was now almost as well-to-do as Abel Frake.

"Because if he's the best hog, Abel, he'll never win the sweepstakes. If a hog, or a man, ever got what he was entitled to once, the eternal stars would quit making melody in their spheres, and all that. You have him about third or fourth best, Abel, and you'll do better, mark my words."

The loafers looked at each other and grinned. Abel smiled his thoughtful, almost wistful, smile and slapped the Storekeeper gently on the shoulder. "I'm going to have that hog in the finest shape I can possibly get him into, and never fear but what if he's the best he'll get the prize. Those men from Ames know their hogs."

"All right," said the Storekeeper, with humorous gloom, "but did you ever hear about automobile wrecks? Did you ever hear about lightning? Did you ever hear about earthquakes or hog cholera or Acts of God? Suppose—as you're supposing, *I* don't suppose it—the judges should be good judges and suppose, even, they should be honest. What about hurricanes? Don't you get that hog too good."

Abel Frake laughed and took a cigar, which he

10

had been fingering gently for some minutes, out of his coat pocket. "Guess I better smoke this," he said. "I've been looking forward to smoking these cigars, and now you've got me into the idea that probably they won't be much good. If they ain't you've got to take the other two back."

"Cigars," said the Storekeeper, "are something else. Providence has to keep its hands off cigars. If that cigar isn't a comfort and an inspiration, it'll only be because a tidal wave fell on it between Havana and here." The Storekeeper thought only in major catastrophes.

Abel split the tip of the cigar with an expert squeeze—the Storekeeper had shown him that trick —and lit it from the match which the Storekeeper held. He let the smoke curl up under his nose and smiled. He sighed with contentment.

"All right," he said, "you've taught me ways of prodigality and waste. You're the kind of a man that would lead a poor farmer to his ruin with your three-for-a-quarter cigars."

"Just as well be ruined one way as another," said the Storekeeper calmly. "If you didn't spend it on cigars you'd probably spend it on Bible tracts to annoy heathen, or for orphanages to soothe the consciences of people who don't want to be bothered looking out for orphans. You might even spend it on slop for that hog of yours. Aren't you going to permit yourself a little indulgence now and then? Are you going to spend your life seeing that that animated lard can astonishes civilization with the world's largest sausage-casings?"

Abel frowned at the Storekeeper. "Call me all the names you want to, but don't say anything against that hog. I've got faith in my hog. I believe in my hog."

"Yes," said the Storekeeper, "if there was anything lacking to beat your But-for-the-grace-of-God-shoat I suppose what you've just said would do it. I suppose he's so fat and mean-natured now that nothing could possibly keep him from being the best hog at the show. Well, that's Item One. Item Two, you're all set on him, so he's just as good as beat this very minute."

Abel Frake laughed deep in his throat, but quietly. "Blue Boy is the best Hampshire boar that ever breathed, right now. And, what's more, the judges will say so."

The Storekeeper looked at him thoughtfully. "They don't always work any way you could see

Them. Your pig might win the prize, but your house would burn down or you'd catch rheumatism. You can't get away from Them."

Every one within miles of Brunswick understood "Them" so well that there was no question. Abel Frake grinned at the Storekeeper.

"I'll make you a little bet. I'll bet you I go to the State Fair, and I'll bet you that Blue Boy wins sweepstakes, and I'll bet you my house doesn't burn down and that we all have a good time and are better off for it when the whole Fair is over."

"Abel," said the Storekeeper solemnly, "if you'd asked me I'd have given you ten to one. But you didn't ask me. I'm one to profit from a fellowman's misfortunes; so I'll bet you. And I bet you that if I lose, something will've happened that we don't know about but that will be worse than anything you can think of. They're tricky."

Abel laughed. "But that way you can't lose. If we don't know of anything that happened, then you can just say that something happened we don't know about. How do I win?"

"If we don't learn about it by a couple of months after Fair time, I'll pay. I don't think They'll bother so much with you."

"It's a bet then."

"It's a bet," said the Storekeeper, gravely and confidently, as though he had just bet on the rising of the sun. "I started me a little Fool Fund Wednesday. I got five dollars in it already and this will make ten."

"Fool Fund! What's that?"

"People think I'm a fool because I've got a notion of what things are all about. So I've begun to capitalize on that opinion. I took the Kellogg-Birge man from Keokuk for five dollars—the first five."

The loafers all laughed expectantly, for a story which they had already heard several times and liked, and Abel asked, "How did you do that?"

"Well, he came in here, and I said something about Hoover was going to be reëlected because there was no one in the country more markedly and preëminently unfitted for public office, and so he was a safe bet. This traveling-man said I was crazy about Hoover being reëlected and I was also crazy in general because there is a destiny that shapes our ends. So I made him a little bet and won five dollars."

"What was the bet?"

The Storekeeper looked mildly bored. "I said if you was driving nails in a board and reaching behind you for the nails, it would be arranged so that you would pick up more of the nails by the point, and have to turn them over, than you would pick up by the head end so that you could drive them without any trouble. Out of a hundred nails."

"Tell him how it come out," said one of the loafers who had heard a dozen times at least.

"It came out seventy-three to twenty-seven, so I took the money."

Abel laughed. "I'm glad you won five dollars so easy, because it will make me feel better about taking your money after the Fair. Your Fool Fund is going to wind up with no assets and no liabilities just two months after Fair Week."

The Storekeeper shook his head. "Except for the five dollars, which any one in the general merchandising business can use, I sure hope so."

There was a faint flurry at the front of the store. "Abel! Do you suppose we ought to be getting back? The Hired Man went over to Pittsville and there isn't a soul on the place."

"Took his wife and kids over to the moving picture," Abel explained to the loafers—even such simple things were worthy of explanation. "I think it's worth while for him to get out occasionally."

He moved up to the front of the store and the Storekeeper followed him. The loafers settled down to another hour of conversation before the Storekeeper's closing time.

"Good night!"

"Good night, Mrs. Frake. You got your sack of candy?"

"Never fear I'd forget that." She went out, laughing.

Brunswick lay on the banks of the Des Moines River seven miles from Pittsville, the county-seat, and fifteen miles from Farmview, the much larger county-seat of the adjoining county. It was almost nine thirty when Abel Frake started for his home, three miles from the tiny town on the way to Pittsville. It was fifteen minutes later when his son, Wayne, just out of the first show of the Farmview movie, drove down the road between the fifteen or twenty scattered houses of Brunswick and pulled up at the Storekeeper's gas stand. He honked twice and the Storekeeper came out.

"Hello, Wayne. Hello, Eleanor. Your folks left here about fifteen minutes ago—and you've still got to take your girl home. You'll catch the dickens! Don't know what the younger generation is coming to, staying out till almost sunset, Saturday evening. How many gallons?"

"Well," said Wayne, "how many gallons d'you think we ought to have, Eleanor?"

Eleanor laughed and then answered rather seriously, "I suppose I ought to get home. Daddy's probably raising the deuce about me this minute. By the time you drive me over to Pittsville and then come back four miles to your house, maybe you'll have about all the driving you want for one evening, Wayne. I ought to do some reading tomorrow."

Although he could not make out one feature of her face, the Storekeeper could see its white oval, turned doubtfully to Wayne, and catch a golden glint as her yellow hair caught a sparkle of light from the bright windows.

"Reading? What for? I thought you were taking a vacation from college!"

"I'm trying to get enough stuff in my head to get extra credits next year and shorten the agony. I suppose I ought to get back—"

"All right. Five gallons." Wayne's voice was slightly cool and the Storekeeper opened the gasoline tank on the car without a word, turned the pump, and said, "Good night, folks." Both answered him and the car shot away.

Although the day had been inhumanly hot, comfort now came from the river and the dewy hills. The planks of the old Brunswick bridge rattled under the little car. They heard the low lifting and falling swell of the river against the piers as they drove on toward the formidable curtain of green blackness at the far approach. Wayne drove with his attention all upon the narrow strip of road disclosed by the lights. The car whipped around the end of the steep approach and settled down quietly upon the smooth, quiet sand road to Pittsville.

They had gone perhaps a mile when she touched his arm with hers and said, "Why are you so quiet?"

He took his time, guiding the little automobile up a long, slippery clay slope before he answered, "Am I quiet? Well, Eleanor, what do you want me to say?"

She laughed nervously. "But you're so different from what you were coming from Farmview. You can be fun when you want to, Wayne. You were fun then."

He shot her an oblique look. "I hope your father won't mind if I keep you out until ten o'clock. We're making good time now. You'll be home by ten." The car slipped by an entrance pillared with poplars and he saw a light in his mother's room.

Again she caught his arm. "Wayne! What's the matter with you?"

He turned his arm away from her, avoiding a small wash in the road. "Well, Eleanor, I guess we might as well have it out. I'm not going up to college until next fall; so I suppose I'm still pretty ignorant. But you were different when you went away last year. I suppose I took a lot for granted just because we went together in high school—"

"Oh, Wayne!" She laughed, and she was conscious that the laugh was not successful. "I'm only seventeen—you're only eighteen. We don't have to be so serious yet. It's a nice evening—why do you take it so to heart that I've been a year up at Iowa State Teachers?"

He did not look to see a flicker of merriment and of curiosity in her eyes. "Not me," he said soberly. "You!"

"I?" She studied for a moment and then she be-

gan to hum a song. At last she patted his shoulder
gently. "Maybe you're right. I hope it's not I."
The car turned at the corner of Mile Lane and
drove straight toward the scattered lights—electric
lights—of Pittsville. The boy's mood slowly wore
off in the fresh night air, under a moon which
fought off the rich, smothering darkness. The road
ran straight and wide and fragrant in front of
them.

His arm—strong and well-rounded, she could
feel—fell around her shoulders. As they came under the clump of black-cherries at the end of the
lane, the car slowed—

"No, Wayne!"

"What's the matter?"

"Wayne, I'm afraid. I—I like you—but I don't
know—I—I don't know—please, Wayne, don't be
mad—"

He turned the Pittsville corner of Mile Lane
without a word and drove down the outermost
street of the town, bringing the car up sharply at
the great Victorian house where she lived. He
threw the door open and helped her to step down
from the roadster.

"Good night," he said.

"Wayne!"

He gave the car a half turn and backed. "What's the matter?"

Her voice was low, but clear and honest. "I want to be friends."

He stared down at the steering-wheel. "Well, aren't we friends?"

She hesitated. "Aren't we?"

"What's the matter with me?" he burst out suddenly. "Or what's the matter with you? Did you meet some man schoolma'am up at that teachers college? Or did you just get educated to the point where I don't interest you any more?"

"That's a silly question. If you didn't interest me any more, why should I have spent all these evenings with you? Oh, Wayne, I don't know what's the matter—" Her tone was vague and evidently perplexed. She stood quietly beside the driveway, slender and troubled, and a sudden access of tenderness made him leap from the car.

"Eleanor! You can tell me the truth." He threw his arms about her, his arms moved beyond his own volition. "You don't need—"

"Oh!" She gasped with evident pain. "You hurt me, Wayne—I'm sorry." Then she laughed, pushing with both arms against his chest. "You're so strong you don't realize—you're like a bear."

"All right," he said sullenly and took a step back toward the car.

"Wayne! Don't—I'm afraid of this love-making —and you hurt me—I didn't think. Wayne, we're so young—"

"I'm older than I was when you went away."

She sighed, her hand at her bosom. "There's still lots of time for—all that. You've got to go through college—and of course, I've got to finish, too."

With the intuition of the very young he guessed at something of what was behind her words and his handsome, boyish face grew still darker.

"Then there's some fellow up there who's— older?"

This trifle of perspicacity made Eleanor angry. She threw back her head and he could see the whiteness of her throat in the moonlight.

"I don't know why you should think that you have a right to ask me such things. I'm not a farm that you can put a mortgage on—" The roar of the engine drowned out the end of her sentence.

When the car had turned the corner of Mile

22

Lane, Eleanor stared after it for a moment doubt-fully. Then she put her hand to her breast tenta-tively, discovered that it was bruised but intact, shrugged her shoulders, and disappeared in the great farm-house at Pittsville's boundary.

By the time Wayne Frake had reached the lane of poplars and white elms that led from the road to the big brick house above the river, he had traveled around the world twice and had become a cosmopolite with iron-gray hair and sad, cynical eyes which women found irresistible. The most famous actress of the day had been his mistress for a year and had attempted to commit suicide when he accepted a commission as the leader of the Czar-ist forces against the Bolsheviki.

He had forgotten her quickly, however, after the success of the Czarist revolution, and particularly when the beautiful daughter of a daughter of the Czar, who had somehow escaped the Bolsheviki, of-fered him her hand and a throne as a reward for the achievements of his incomparable military tal-ents, and particularly for his bravery at the decisive battle of—of Slavootski. He had refused, of course, but ah, those evenings and nights in the great palace above the Volga! At least the blood of Wayne Frake would sometime sit upon the throne of Peter the Great and reign over the Russias!

Himself, like General Krack (whose exploits, by some coincidence, he had that evening seen in a moving-picture version at Farmview) must always be a lone, wandering soul, seeking for absinthe. (Was it absinthe? The hell with these details!) Then there was the great reception when he returned to visit his aged parents living near Brunswick, a small village in the southeastern part of Iowa. For the first time, New York's witty mayor found himself outdone in graceful and sophisticated repartee. Then there was the slow drive up Wall Street, Broadway, and Fifth Avenue while cheers rang and ticker tape streamed down from the buildings.

Should Eleanor see him at the parade or should he save her for the second triumph in Pittsville? He slowed the Ford a trifle. It would never do to reach home just as he was coming to the best part.

As the Rolls-Royce moved past the City Hall, under the windows of the Stock Exchange, he chanced to glimpse a familiar face at the curb— well, on a person at the curb. He would know that lovely heart-shaped chin anywhere. "Can we swing a little closer to the curb?" he asked Al Smith and the Mayor, who were sitting with him in the car. They swung out of the line of march for a moment.

"Hello, Eleanor." His eyes rested for a moment amusedly on the spare, gaunt figure of the dyspeptic man beside her, with his thin, severe face and his thick-lensed, horn-rimmed glasses. Two equally thin, dyspeptic children clung to each hand—they, too, wore horn-rimmed glasses. Should he smile disdainfully? No, he could be generous. The car drove on.

Just in time. Wayne pulled up beside another car in the carriage-yard.

It was Harry Ware's powerful little roadster and in it, Wayne knew quite well, he could find not only Harry Ware but Margy Frake. Lucky kids! There would never be any quarrels or heartbreaks for them.

"Hullo, Wayne!"

"Hello, Harry," he replied with dignity and a touch of melancholy, as became the recent General Wayne Krack Frake.

"The folks are in bed, asleep; don't wake them," said Margy, less considerate than considering.

"I? Why should I wake them?" asked the late General W. K. Frake, annoyed at the implication of clumsiness. He strode off with a step which Harry and Margy thought rather peculiar.

"A little bit loony, our Wayne," said Margy, who was one year her brother's senior in years and, being female, at least five years more mature.

Harry Ware's roadster had been in the carriage-yard for a long time when Wayne's car came in. Margy and Harry had left the Pittsville dance early because the evening was hot, because the orchestra was not much good, because there were mosquitoes, because the Pittsville crowd was not very congenial, because the dance floor had been skimpily waxed— but chiefly they had left because both felt an urge for that seclusion which is the aim and the privilege of the reflective and the philosophical.

When Wayne drove in Margy and Harry had decided:

1. That there is probably life on the larger stars. (Their data on stellar temperatures being limited.)

2. That there is probably a heaven, because after all . . .

3. That every one ought to go to Europe once, but going all the time is an affectation.

4. That fish never know what caught them.

5. That how can people read that stuff of Edgar Guest's?

At the moment of Wayne's arrival they were engaged in the most fascinating topic of all:

6. That if Margy ever married any one and thereafter had a son, should it take its father's whole name and thus be, let us say, John Harrison Doe, Jr., or should it take its father's first name and the Frake middle name, thus becoming John Frake Doe?

Margy contended stoutly that "Junior" was distinguished, and that the name of any exceptional male who fathered her child should be perpetuated in its entirety; Harry argued, on the other hand, that Frake was a fine old name which should be continued as well on the distaff side of the family as on whatever side the other side happened to be.

The amiability of the argument was exceptional. The conditional subjunctive was carefully maintained by Margy and respected by Harry. A pleasant variant was introduced when Harry suggested that if Margy should ever marry any one and thereafter have a baby, the outcome might be a girl, in which case it should be named for its mother, Margharita Frake Doe. Margy felt that it might very well be

27

named for its paternal grandmother—say, Mary Smith Doe. There were excellent arguments to support both propositions.

Wayne paused by the car briefly.

Conversation languished a trifle after the boy had left. The man started several remarks which faded out. Margy, her chin on her hand, simply stared through the wind-shield at the dark silhouette of the trees in the hill pasture. A cicada which had been completely ignored during the first part of the evening now became painfully audible. Both felt the urge to begin one of those intimate conversations which start in more sophisticated societies with, "But now, candidly—" but neither knew the word.

"How does it happen you're not going to the Fair, Harry?"

He smiled at her. "Just this minute I'm saving every nickel. When we get married this fall, I want to see a little bit of the world before we have children to stop us. I thought we'd take the car to New York and then maybe, if I can save enough, go over to Europe and see whatever there is over there to see. Of course, we couldn't go till early winter when everything was finished up around the farm. If we had as much as a nickel left when we got back we could stay in New York a week or two and see some shows and stay once at a big hotel and see how it would be to be rich."

"But what," Margy asked, "are you going to do if I don't marry you?"

He looked at her soberly. "Margy, for ten years I've never made any plan except with you in it. I don't know what I'd do. It wouldn't make much difference."

His tone was so earnest that she was touched. "That would be a nice honeymoon," she said gently and laughed. "I might almost marry you just to get to go along."

Suddenly she was so close to him, gathered in his arms. She pressed his head down and he kissed her upon the cheeks and eyes, and upon her eager lips.

"No," he whispered, "not to go with me, but to be with me. You'll marry me because you want me —because you love me." His hands wandered to her bosom and she trembled and waited.

He released her slowly and left her somehow famished after having gazed upon plenty. Margy began to cry. He had held her too intimately or not intimately enough and she suddenly felt shame that she had encouraged him—to what, she was not sure, but to more than he had cared to take.

Instantly he was alarmed, solicitous. "What's the matter, Margy dear? You wanted me to, didn't you? Why are you crying? It's all right—we're going to be married to-morrow—or just as soon as you get back from the State Fair, anyway. And then we're going—"

Starving, enraged, she was almost as much surprised by her next words as he was. "We're never going to be married."

He attempted to put his arms about her again and she struck at him fiercely. "Margy!"

"How do you dare to manhandle me like that? You hurt me! I told you I wouldn't even tell you whether I'd marry you or not until after the State Fair! And you do things like that! Well, I know about you now. I'm not ever going to marry you. You won't have to wait till after State Fair to know, now."

Outraged and astonished, he dimly suspected his offense. He smothered the angry retort that rushed to his lips and said quietly, "Anyway, I'll wait."

"Oh, the hell with all that! You make me sick

and tired. I knew I didn't want to marry you all the time, but you moaned around so that I tried to think I loved you. Now I know that you're—an animal. I don't ever want to see you again." She jumped down from the car. "That's all—everything."

She stared at him for a moment, sobbing. A little smile touched the corners of his strong, gentle mouth. "Anyway," he repeated, "I'll wait." The roadster backed out of the carriage-yard.

SUNDAY MORNING

CHAPTER II

SUNDAY MORNING

"No HAWG," said the Hired Man, "is ever pleased."
He uttered this opinion in reply to a remark of
Abel Frake's about Blue Boy's customary feeding-
time fight with an imaginary interloper. Blue Boy
had rushed out from his cool and muddy wallow,
under the shade of the barn, with fire in his eye,
when he heard the mash being poured into his
trough.

First the monstrous mushroom of fat nosed up
and down the trough, partly to be sure that there
were no strange noses in it, partly to select the spot
at which the wholly homogeneous mixture was
most delicious. Quieting down, after a few bitter
remarks and casual curses, to his eating, he slowly
pushed a non-existent adversary down the trough
to the very end; then with his body parallel to the
trough, he put one leg in his breakfast to be sure
that the scoundrel should not get in at the other
end. His blue-black coat bristled with menace to

Abel and the Hired Man and the world of hogs. This was Blue Boy's slop and by God he would have every drop of it.

Abel watched Blue Boy's daily miracle of absorption with quiet satisfaction. "Sure pointing up. He's half again the hog he was last year. They'll have to go some if they get the sweepstakes away from him this time. What do you think, Eph?" It was the thousandth time in the past few months that he had asked.

"Hell! didn't that Crawford sow throw the damnedest litter by him that was ever thrown in this county? Look at that!" He kicked Blue Boy solidly, between the bars of the fence. Blue Boy swore at him indifferently. "Let me tell you, that's all pig— that's solid."

"Well, we've still got twenty-four hours to go before the Fair. Hope he doesn't get adenoids. Come on in the house, Eph. The kids ought to be through breakfast and I want to go over the week's work."

As they neared the house the clinking of china told them that the washing of the breakfast dishes was already in progress. Wayne was repairing a chair in the back yard, but he dropped it as he saw

36

his father and Eph approach. The Hired Man sat down on a bench on the back porch and slipped a chew of fine-cut into his mouth; Wayne sat down beside him.

"You can cut the sixteen acres down by the old brick-yard and the twelve of clover up by the Drummond corner to-morrow, Eph. Tuesday you go into the alfalfa. Wednesday, if it's nice, you can rake. Thursday you can start with the new fence up on the hill corn-field. Friday, and Saturday morning, you'll put in the hay. I'm going to fix Blue Boy's crate."

In the kitchen, Melissa was making a low objection to Fate. "I wouldn't have cared if it had broken in camp, at State Fair time. I *planned* for it to get broken then. Something always gets broken then and I thought this would be it. It got cracked camping two years ago and I counted on it to last out." She looked ruefully at the two pieces of broken stoneware cup in her hand.

"But Mother—how could you *plan*—?"

"Margy, you have to plan—everything. I've got the whole Fair planned right now. If you're careful you can make everything you want come out the way you want it to. I always have." She pointed through the dining-room to a picture in a tremendous gilt frame which hung against the back wall. Margy sighed premonitorily.

"Did I ever tell you the story about your great-grandmother Margharita—?"

"Yes, Mother, a hundred times!"

"You're named for her," Mrs. Frake continued placidly. "Well, when your great-grandfather came here there were Indians, there were even Indians camped in the grove down by the river. So one night some of the braves got drunk and came up and told your great-grandmother they wanted more whisky. Do you want to know what she did?"

"No, Mother, I already know. She took her broom—"

"She took her broom and she chased those Indians clear down to the River Road."

"But, Mother, how could she plan that?"

Mrs. Frake, a little uncertain of the application of the story, but glad to have gotten the classic of her mother's mother in once more, merely sighed. "You're young yet, daughter. You'll understand all of these things when you get older—Frakes always plan.—What's the matter with you to-day?

Sunday Morning

You almost dropped your father's coffee-cup!"

"I don't know. I guess I'm just bored."

Mrs. Frake smiled and Margy faintly resented her mother's matronly comeliness and her placidity. "Well, it's State Fair time. I guess I get a little restless myself about this time of year.—Now, you take the scraps and go out and feed the chickens."

Margy particularly hated chickens. They had ugly manners, they had peevish dispositions quite unlike her own ordinary smiling calm, they were filthy, cruel, lascivious creatures in feeding and in all aspects of their domestic life. She hated them unusually to-day because behind the cackling irritation of the hens she recognized something that was not wholly incompatible with the mood which had lately grown upon her. So she took a particular pleasure in spilling the scraps over three or four of the noisiest hens and watching the other chickens peck them.

After he had eaten, Wayne made some dim remark about readjusting the timer on the Ford and strayed out to the old carriage-house, now the garage. Abel hurried to the barn and Blue Boy's crate. No one could plane a joint or turn a screw for that crate but Abel, whose clever hands had learned all the tricks of woodworking from his father, a cabinet-maker in his leisure moments.

The tradition of knowing several trades had come from New England to Pennsylvania, from Pennsylvania to Ohio and from Ohio to Iowa with the family, and Abel hammered his own iron corner-elbows at a little forge, in the corner of the shop away from the hay-loft overhang.

Restless beyond endurance, Margy danced across the lawn to the garage. Her mother was darning stockings; there was not much to do in a well-managed farm-house on Sunday. There was a little fun to be had with Wayne—he had had either a devil of a fight or an unusual success with Eleanor the evening before, and Margy intended to discover which. She had not been able to interpret the dignity of his gait as he crossed the lawn last night.

The garage was very quiet. Then she heard a voice. "Now, Mister, I'll take that ormolyew clock over there." There was a reedy click, and then her brother's voice again, coldly, exultant. "Ah, nailed it, Mister. Now then, I think I'll take that pearl-handled revolver—oh, I know it ain't any good, but it cost more than a dime and it will be all right to give to some kid." Again the reedy click, again the exultant voice. "Well, now, I think I'll just look the layout over. I can get anything I want, Mister, never doubt that—"

Margy peered through a crack and saw her brother flourishing what she plainly recognized as one of her mother's round embroidery hoops. At the end of the shed there was a block of wood, up-ended, and flat on top of it was a small sawn lozenge of wood, perhaps six inches in diameter and two inches thick. As she watched, Wayne tossed the embroidery hoop expertly and it encircled the lozenge so exactly that it hardly vibrated as it settled into place on the block.

Margy opened the door and walked in. "What in the world are you up to, Wayne Frake, with Mother's embroidery hoop?"

The boy tossed the embroidery hoop into the corner indifferently. "Oh, it's just a game. I found the hoop out here and I was trying to toss it over that piece of wood there."

"But I heard you talking."

"Well, can't a fellow talk a little?" He had turned

41

crimson, she observed with satisfaction. "I'd better talk to myself than to some people I know in our house. What are you doing out here? You ought to be in helping Mother. I've got to fix this car. You get out, you're no help."

" 'Now I think I'll take that pearl-handled revolver, Mister,' " the female Frake mimicked.

"Oh, so you were standing out there listening? Well, I wouldn't do a lot of talking if I were you. Do you want to know what time you came in from Harry Ware's automobile last night?"

"I know very well what time I came in from Harry Ware's automobile. Do you want to know why you were strutting so funny across the yard last night, after you took Eleanor home?"

She realized after she had said it that it had a sinister sound, but she was not prepared for the fury on her brother's face. "I suppose you'd have your own ideas on that! Don't judge others by yourself."

Both were silent, shocked at the intimations that their own lips had released. There was not a sound for a minute—two minutes—

"Buddy, I'm sorry. I didn't mean what I said any more than you meant what you said."

"Gee, I'm glad you said that, Margy. Of course

42

I didn't mean it. If I'd say a thing like that and mean it I ought to go shoot myself. I'll tell you what all this is," he added generously. "It's a hoop-la stand—see?"

She stared. "A hoop-la stand? What's that?"

He examined her face closely to make certain that her mood was as candid as his own. Then the deep-grained, cynical suspicions of which youth is savagely capable before it has been led astray by civic club mottoes, halted the declaration he had been about to make. He turned away indifferently. "It's a kind of a game," he said.

Margy laughed. "You *are* crazy." She surveyed the carriage-house and looked indifferently at the roadster.

"What's Eleanor doing these days, Bud?" She tried to make the inquiry completely casual; she was almost successful.

"I don't know what Eleanor's doing; I don't care what she's doing."

"Oh, you two had a fight?"

He lowered at her. "Can't a fellow take a girl driving a few times without his own folks thinking he's going to marry her right away? What's Harry Ware doing these days? And these evenings?"

43

Margy laughed good-naturedly. "I didn't know you had a fight. I'm sorry, Bud. You were so funny last night when you came home. I wondered—"

"Why was I so funny?"

"Well, you were kind of stalking across the yard. Harry thought you were walking a little bit funny, too—it wasn't just me."

Wayne lifted the hood of the roadster and began to trifle with various nuts, rods, and set-screws. For a long time the faint rattling that he made was the only sound in the shed. By and by his sister spoke to him again.

"Bud."

"Yes?"

"Sometimes don't you feel like you'd like to go away somewhere and just raise hell—about everything?"

Bud frowned. Profanity was the prerogative of men in the part of the world in which he lived. "I don't know what you mean."

Margy's full bosom drew her dress up as she shrugged. "I guess you wouldn't, Farmer Frake. But Eleanor would—don't ever doubt that." She swung open the small door of the carriage-house and dashed across the lawn to the back porch. Wayne stared after her with mixed annoyance and bewilderment. Girls are crazy, he finally decided, and picked up the embroidery ring.

In the house, Margy's mother was seated on the sofa, almost completely surrounded by piles of sewing. She was beautiful in the lavish, friendly, domestic way in which the women of Rembrandt and Rubens are beautiful, thus poised, empress of her own generous affairs—but Margy did not notice that.

Margy pulled up a chair and sat down patiently to help her.

"I don't know how I get so behind on this," said Mrs. Frake. "It seems to me that every Fair time I'm always about a year behind on my mending."

Margy sewed in silence. Mrs. Frake made several further tentative remarks and then she dropped her sewing upon her knee. "Margy," she said, "what in the world is the matter with you?"

"Nothing's the matter with me. Why do you ask that?"

"You seem so different to-day, and I've seen it

45

coming on for weeks. What have you got worrying you? Frakes don't worry about anything."

"There's nothing the matter with me!" Margy began to cry and retired to her bedroom. Mrs. Frake shook her head and placidly continued her sewing.

NIGHT JOURNEY

CHAPTER III

NIGHT JOURNEY

As ONE who carefully arranged life in the precise patterns which she selected, Mrs. Frake felt that the Iowa State Fair had probably been put off a few days too many. She very well knew the tensions and the urgencies of the week before the event, but this year it seemed to her that that final suspense had broken; that—if she had been a member of a boxing commission—her family was overtrained for the Fair.

For six days Wayne had been growling and sulking, and for six days Margy had been sulking and weeping on the very slightest pretexts—or on no pretext at all. Just—as Wayne protested—bawling.

Mrs. Frake had actually been too busy to be very much disturbed by these phenomena. Reflections on her own youth and observations of her children had taught her that the emotions of younger persons are very curious, very changeable, and not particu-

larly important, outside of humanitarian consider-
ations. So she had carefully estimated the number
of days that butter for the trip could be expected
to keep in Mason jars, and let these other, probably
intricate and unreasonable affairs take care of
themselves.

Abel Frake had been too preoccupied with Blue
Boy to notice anything of less than seismic consequence. Blue Boy had pointed up so considerately
that it seemed that he would reach the very needle-
point of his condition just as he lifted his snout at
the judges in the stock pavilion at Des Moines. If
Blue Boy proved to be the best Hampshire boar in
Iowa, it followed that he would be the best Hampshire boar in the world. He would take the Interna-
tional sweepstakes at Chicago and Abel Frake, pros-
perous but obscure farmer and stock-breeder of
Brunswick, Iowa, would be known far and wide as
the owner of the finest hog in the universe. More-
over, Blue Boy's facile amours would be worth—
whatever they were worth to him—a very substantial sum of money to Abel Frake.

"I wish I hadn't broken that cracked cup," Mrs.
Frake told Margy, worriedly, when the tent, the
canned provisions, the cooking utensils, the bed-

ding, the linen, the clothes, were all packed beside Blue Boy's crate on the farm truck. "Now I've got to take one of the new set. One cup always gets cracked and it will be just my luck to have it be that one to break up the six."

The whole farm was crackling with preparation. The Hired Man had not marcelled Blue Boy, but only because the curl of the hair was not a judging point. He had manicured him; he had viewed more critically than a Corot the misty sunrise tint of his snout; no Park Avenue specialist knew one half about any dowager's bowels what the Hired Man knew about Blue Boy's—in addition, the Hired Man was pleased with what he knew; Blue Boy's coat was curried and rubbed to enameled perfection; Blue Boy's tail was curled so tightly that its tension would have alarmed uninformed persons; Blue Boy, as he lay and rocked upon his four legs, was the finest creature of his species that had ever existed in time and space.

Sunday passed quietly. Mrs. Frake had managed things so well that there was really nothing much to do on the day before the departure. Late in the morning the Storekeeper drove over with the last of the supplies which the family would need for Fair

Week. While the family leaned on the fence he sat in his little Ford truck and talked.

"I wouldn't depend on this fine weather. If you'd get off right away you'd be sure to get to Ottumwa before it begins to rain."

Abel Frake tapped the ash off of one cigar of the box which the Storekeeper had given him, explaining that the five dollars would cover it easily. "The paper says continued fair."

"Listen, Abel," said the Storekeeper, more conspicuously patient than ever, "what would you say about the weather, yourself?"

Abel looked at the skies, familiarly. "I'd say it was going to be good weather. A little bit hot but clear."

"You see?" said the Storekeeper triumphantly. "That's what I'd say myself. Bet a cigar there'll be a thunder-storm yet this afternoon."

At noon the rain began and by three o'clock the family had heard lightning hit the rods twice. At four o'clock the black matted clouds began to split; at five o'clock the sun shone brightly. Blue Boy could not start until sunset at any rate, for he must not suffer and sweat in the heat.

The family waited beside the truck. Slowly the

sun moved down until the ferocity of its heat was sensibly diminished. Mrs. Frake served the family with sandwiches from the first of three lunch kits she had prepared. There was hot coffee from the kitchen stove, there were some of her own cucumber, green tomato and onion pickles—the jars dotted with cloves, mace, whole black pepper and bay leaf.

A little later the sun had definitely set and Abel went around the house trying the doors and windows. The sky was rich with the sunset. There was a warm light over everything. It was with almost an eery feeling that the family settled itself into the truck—Abel, his wife, Margy in the big front seat; Wayne back on the folded tent and the bedding near the boar.

They looked back at the house and Abel tramped on the starter. The motor burst into an even grumble and Abel turned around the carriage-yard carefully. The Hired Man, his wife and his three children were lined up by the side of the driveway. As the truck turned its nose into the face of the disappearing sun they suddenly burst into frenzied shouts and wavings of the arms.

"Hooray! Hooray!" they shouted. "Ray,"

53

shouted the three-year-old, running around in circles until she fell, laughing.

"Hooray for Blue Boy! Blue Boy!"

The family laughed and waved at the Hired Man's family.

"Oink!" said Blue Boy.

The familiar river road toward Brunswick suddenly seemed strange because at this time it led to strange and romantic places. When the truck passed Brunswick, the Storekeeper and the loafers, who had evidently set out scouts, suddenly rushed out from the store porch with cheers and admonitions.

"Bring him back with the bacon or as it," yelled the Storekeeper, who was sometimes capable of a classic reference.

The shouts died out behind them. The dusk had come upon the truck as it left Brunswick on the less familiar road to Ottumwa.

Mrs. Frake coughed. "I think I caught a little cold, Wednesday, when I took down the washing in the rain."

Abel Frake, guiding the car, took one hand from the wheel to pat her. "Take anything for it?"

"No, it didn't seem to set in and I hope it's going to pass off."

Night Journey

They passed through Douds, and a little later, through Selma. The new electric lights were burning brilliantly in both places. The truck droned along at ten or twelve miles an hour. Every time that Blue Boy was disturbed, a few ounces were lost from his perfect condition. But the morning would see them pulling up within sight of the great gilded Capitol dome and the shining Fair Grounds. Abel Frake swayed the car over slight inequalities in the surfaced road.

Mrs. Frake coughed. "Maybe we better stop in Eldon and get you something for that cold," Abel suggested.

"Everything'll be closed. It doesn't amount to anything."

They passed through the smoky, dirty little railroad junction without pausing and found themselves again between the clean trees and hedgerows. Abel switched on his lights. Night had officially set in. A golden moon was well up toward the zenith and its light across the sky made all the wooded horizons seem remote and mysterious.

Over the road-bed of an old railroad right-of-way they came into Ottumwa, the principal city of the whole section. To avoid stops and starts which might disturb Blue Boy, Abel picked his way around the back streets of the city to his highway again.

Mrs. Frake coughed. "We'll reach Oskaloosa about midnight, Mama. There'll be some drug-store open all night there where we can get you a little pine syrup. There might even be one open in Eddyville when we go through there."

"I don't want a thing! I'm all right. This cold is wearing off."

Abel Frake drew the car up beside the road and stopped the motor. "How's he coming along, Wayne?"

"He's fine. He's grunting a little at some of the bumps, but I think he's about half asleep. He's not worrying any."

"Good!" Abel dismounted from the high seat of the truck, walked around to the end of the car and inspected the hog. The somnolent animal sighed and gasped, breathed a soft oath and began to snore quietly again. "He's certainly standing the ride fine so far."

Abel started the truck quietly and slipped in the gears so gently that his human passengers hardly realized that they had started to move. Blue Boy, however, protested sharply. As they drove out from Ottumwa the traffic of cars to that city grew more scattered. Finally, they were almost alone upon a road which wound in slow turns and gentle grades between the perfumed hedges and stiff martial ranks of the ripening corn, the yellow light of the moon hanging and flowing upon the road before them.

"How are you doing back there, Wayne?"

Wayne stirred from the pallet of blankets and bedclothes he had made himself on top of Blue Boy's crate, at the sound of his mother's voice. "Oh, fine. Why are you all so quiet?"

"Got to let Blue Boy get his rest," said Abel, turning the car gently around a pit in the concrete. "You got your pickles, Melissa?"

"Here." She pointed at a cardboard carton between her feet. Along the wall of Melissa Frake's kitchen at home was a long row of yellow and red ribbons which she had won for angel's food, devil's food and layer cake; cherry preserves made by the old Stidger recipe which had come down in the family for generations uncounted; for chicken dressing; for raised bread; for doughnuts. There were two blue ribbons—one for candied cherries

57

and for a mincemeat to which Mrs. Frake had sur-
reptitiously added some sherry wine the doctor had
once prescribed as a tonic for Margy.

The little bit that was left over, it seemed a shame
to waste. The judges awarded Mrs. Frake's mincemeat a blue ribbon with a promptness and una-
nimity which had shocked her. Although she felt a
very small twinge of conscience when she saw this
blue ribbon, she felt somehow that she had won it
fairly. She also felt a slight moral indignation
against judges whose souls would not warn them of
irreligious matters in mincemeat.

This year she had concocted pickles of such intricate and overwhelming delicacy that she hoped for
another blue ribbon to add to the row. She had
never entered pickles before. However, she realized
that pickles were a small matter as compared with
Blue Boy.

"Think they'll ride all right there?"

"They'll have a chance to settle before the judges
see them. Besides, they're packed tight, in layers."

The truck struck the brick paving of Eddyville.
Already many of the houses were dark, but from
their by-road they could see the glow of Main
Street. Again there were cars and companionship

upon the road. After this, they realized, it would be a solitary drive, for it was nearly nine o'clock. Driving alone in time as their forefathers had driven in the space of the Iowa prairies, they felt a faint sense of adventure and the large *Sehnsucht* of a starry, slightly humid Iowa night.

"What are you thinking about, Margy?"

"I'm not thinking about anything. I wish we were there. I wish it was morning."

Mrs. Frake laughed comfortably. "We'll be there soon enough. And then there'll be plenty to do. You'd better try to get some sleep, you and Wayne."

"How can I sleep here, squashed between you and Papa?"

"Why don't you go back with Wayne?" Abel asked. "There's plenty of room on top of that crate and he's got some kind of a bed fixed up there."

"And sleep over that hog? No, thank you."

Abel laughed. "That's a special hog. It isn't everybody that gets a chance to sleep on the crate of a hog like that. Besides, he's been washed and curried till he's probably cleaner than any of us. We've been washed, but we haven't been curried."

"I don't like hogs," said Margy, decisively.

"Well," said her father, "maybe hogs don't like you, either, but you don't hear Blue Boy making a big fuss because you're riding in his car."

Now the farm-houses at each side of the road were frequently unlighted and relays of cicadas which lined all the roads from Brunswick to Des Moines could be heard above the even hum of the motor. A glimpse of another car upon the road was a rarity now, and a subject for speculation. The moon, last light of humanity, was sinking in the east.

The slow, droning truck seemed hardly to move, yet they had already come more than forty miles. Wayne stirred from his blankets in the back of the truck and sat bolt upright. "I can't sleep."

"It's a fact," his mother said. "It's my bedtime but I don't feel the least bit sleepy. It seems as if we were the last people left in the world and we had to watch it. Ah, we're going west now! See the Big Dipper?"

"How can you tell by that?" Margy asked crossly.

"You don't know that? You take the last two stars in the bowl, and right beyond them, a little to the left, that's the Pole Star. That's north. My grandfather set his fences on that star."

"Doesn't it ever move?"

"Of course not—that's why it's the Pole Star," said Mrs. Frake a little inaccurately. Far ahead, across the hills and valleys, they could see a very faint smudge of light. That was Oskaloosa.

Wayne had subsided into another day-dream. He was imagining Eleanor now, just falling asleep, and laughing at him. For a moment he almost regretted that the State Fair had taken him away from her. They would have fixed everything up. He was sure he could have kissed her good night, if he'd just tried to kiss her good night.

Maybe a good-night kiss didn't seem very important to her. Maybe she had asked a lot of people up at that college to kiss her good night. Maybe they had. He clinched his fist so violently that there was a little pain on the inside of his wrist. The sensation transferred his attentions to his muscles. He felt the hard swelling of his biceps, already building up and down into a solid terraced dome from shoulder to elbow; he felt the cordy firmness of his forearm— if he had them here, the villainous seducers who had

61

kissed Eleanor good night, he would teach them to take advantage of an innocent girl's unsophistication.

Twice he smacked his competent fist into the palm of his left hand. About two licks like that and those male schoolma'ams—

"Was that Blue Boy?"

Wayne grasped frantically for an explanation. "I—I guess I was asleep. I—thought I was having a fight with somebody. What are all of you doing up there?"

"Nothing," his mother answered. "Did you see them turn the lights off over there on that farm?"

"Wonder what they were doing up so late."

"Maybe somebody's sick. Maybe they've got a doctor in."

They were all silent, speculating. And the truck drove on. The night settled down rapidly. Once the moonset in the west had vanished, the darkness dropped down suddenly and blackly and the truck's headlights picked out a way, washed in color, along the dim gray of the Iowa road.

Said Margy timidly, "Maybe somebody's dying. Maybe some woman is having a baby—"

It suddenly occurred to all of them that life went

62

on, far outside their consciousnesses, in many places and at all times.

"Poor soul!" said Mrs. Frake, sympathetically. "If it's a baby I hope it comes right away. And if it's somebody sick that's going to die I hope they die quick."

"I been reading a thing in a magazine," said Wayne, "that proves that time is just a kind of space. You can see up and down and to both sides and in front and behind. This fellow thinks that if we were made different we could see to-morrow and yesterday just the same way—but we don't because we can only see three dimensions. But really, time is just a way of saying a direction we don't know."

Mrs. Frake laughed. "Was he married?"

"I don't know."

"Well, if he was, and he'd ask his wife, he wouldn't go in for such ideas. Time, you can't change. They can figure all they want to on what way twenty minutes from now is from here, but it takes just so long to darn a sock and just so long to bake a cake, and if you're at a fair or a church supper or something, it lasts just so long, no matter how you try to stretch it out."

"I suppose you know better than he does," said Wayne, disrespectfully.

"I guess I do," said Melissa Frake, good-naturedly. "I know better than to waste my time fooling with notions like that."

But Wayne, lying on his back on Blue Boy's crate, was stirred to speculation by the cold, bright, distant stars. After a while he imagined that if you went out toward such and such a star, and then turned a corner, like, you would probably be able to see to-morrow around the bend. The process worked, for the next thing that he saw was to-morrow.

They stopped at a little drug-store in Oskaloosa and bought Mrs. Frake some medicine for her cough. From the drug-store cooler, Abel got fresh cold water for Blue Boy, who was droning sleepily between downright snores and a sense of depression because his barn-lot seemed not so substantial and secure as he had thought it. Sometimes it bumped most objectionably.

"He's riding mighty fine," Abel reported in a subdued voice to Mrs. Frake, who was enjoying her cough syrup.

"He breathes so," said Margy, in a tone of simple

loathing. They passed a little country graveyard, overgrown with weeds and bushes, white and stark enough in the moonlight, but devoid of the dignity and serenity of well-kept country graveyards.

"Looks unappetizing," said Abel Frake, an orderly man.

And so, thought Margy, in a hundred years will my grave look, and there I'll be for good and all and nothing will have been any fun and nothing much ever will have happened. A silly business, living. And somehow she felt that in some manner Harry might have made it less silly, and had withheld something precious from her, selfishly or stupidly. A dim resentment turned vaguely and more vaguely in her mind, growing less tangible at every turn.

"You better take Blue Boy straight to the Stock Pavilion when we get there," said Mrs. Frake. "The youngsters are getting a good sleep and they'll be ready to help get the tent up and straighten things. Then you can take us up and leave us and go back and enter my pickles and tend to Blue Boy. You folks can get a bite at some stand and I'll take a nap before supper-time. After supper, we'll go out and see the Fair."

"No," said Abel, "I'll drop you and the children

first and you can be working on things while I take Blue Boy down. I want you to get a good sleep and clear up that cold of yours. It'd be a shame if you didn't enjoy every minute of the Fair, after waiting for it all these months."

"But it'll make a difference to Blue Boy, standing there while the things are unloaded, and it'll only take a minute to get the crate out. There's always plenty to help around."

"Well," said Abel, uncertainly, "we'll see when we get there. We're making mighty good time now. These concrete roads certainly do make a big difference."

She'd see that they did get the hog off first, Mrs. Frake thought, for the one thing which could crown Fair Week and make its perfect joys ecstatic would be for Abel's hog to win.

Then she and Wayne could pitch the tent and it wouldn't take any time to spread the bedding and get a place to cook fixed outside. Then she could find out where the best grocery stand was and then she could get a little nap and after she woke up—

Only Abel felt the dews which came toward morning and saw the trees faintly begin to silhouette themselves against a dawning gray light. A

66

little later he could see the sunrise from the side door of the truck, and then he began to hear a rising chorus of farm animals from the farms which drifted by the car. Only Abel saw the freshly gilded dome of the Capitol suddenly shine out over Des Moines, and the newly whitewashed Fair Buildings which promised them carnival from the near side of the town. At the gates he halted and showed a sleepy watchman his entry slip for Blue Boy. Mrs. Frake started up.

"Wake up, children," she cried, "wake up! We're here! We're at the Fair!"

MONDAY MORNING

CHAPTER IV

MONDAY MORNING

A few hours later Wayne Frake woke in his section of a divided tent, which was as neatly arranged as Mrs. Frake's kitchen. His mother was already up, for he could hear the crackling of Frake bacon and Frake eggs in a great skillet outside, and the odors were maddening and delightful. A spicy smell of coffee came in with the fresh air under the edge of the tent, lifted for coolness.

He awoke with a sense of suspense retained from the previous evening. There was something he intended to do to-day—ah, yes! This was the day! He jumped to his feet, pulled off his nightshirt and hastily smoothed the covers out to air. Then he pulled on his clothes and hurried down to the baths. The family was awaiting breakfast for him when he returned, bathed and fresh-shaven.

"Did you have to sleep *all* morning?" Margy inquired crossly when he sat down at the camp table. Wayne yawned pretentiously.

"If you'd done any of the heavy work that Mama and I did yesterday you wouldn't be up so early this morning—and you wouldn't be so grouchy." He took a number of fried eggs and an amount of bacon that promised better things for the fall hog market.

Mrs. Frake, somewhat pink and warm, but full of affairs, replenished the platter and put more eggs and bacon on the skillet.

"Don't you two start out fighting," she warned cheerfully. "This is Fair Week and everybody is going to enjoy it if I have to follow them with a shotgun. Did you see Blue Boy this morning, Papa?"

"I was down a while ago, but nobody was up yet. I'm going down as soon as I eat breakfast. They seemed to be taking pretty good care of him last night."

"Did you get my pickles in all right?"

"Yes." Abel Frake grinned. "And don't you worry but the judges will take good care of them, too. I don't know where they get all these starving people for judges."

"Hope they don't poison them." Mrs. Frake's face indicated that she did not think that they would.

72

Monday Morning

Abel looked at his daughter. "What are you young folks going to do?"

"Mama and I are going to the horse-races and to the show this evening in the grand stand. Aren't we, Mama?"

"If I get time," said Mrs. Frake absently. "There's a lot of things that ought to be washed and I'll have to press out the men's suits. You might have to go alone. You wouldn't mind, would you?"

"What are you going to do, Wayne?"

"Oh, I'm just going to look around. I'm going up to the amphitheater and see what kind of samples they're putting out this year. Maybe I'll go on some of the rides, or something."

"Fine," said Abel. "I'll have to keep a close watch on Blue Boy till the judging Wednesday. After that we can all get around together, some."

As soon as breakfast was over, Wayne strode off down the hill from the little tent city that had arisen overnight. Gay, cheaply colored streets stretched off in every direction. It was not probable that the place he was looking for would be where it had been the preceding year, but it was worth while to begin his search there.

Very few of the stands were open so early in the

morning, and in most of those that were open the lessees were merely mixing their lemonade—arranging the dozen or so halved lemons or oranges which would be the whole representation of citrus fruits in their slightly poisonous beverages all day—setting up nets filled with canes, "The cane you ring, gentlemen, is the cane you get"—dusting off kewpie dolls at the wheels of fortune, putting their little stocks of garish novelties at their Coney Island best.

Men with only underwear shirts on above the waist worked at the ropes and stakes of the tents. Late exhibits were still being brought through the gates on trucks. Wayne paused a moment to watch a horseshoe pitching contest which showed promise —one contestant pitched eight double-ringers in succession—but after that it was made too plain that he had been merely lucky.

Some one raised the flag above the Administration Building, a dark brick building which stood on the hill. A sudden din started in the Engineering Hall as switches were turned on thrashers, cream separators, refrigerating devices, truck motors half-cased in glass to show their inner workings, cattle salt presses and the thousand mechanisms which farmers might buy. The Fair had started.

At the place where the hoop-la tent had stood the year before there was a freak tent this year. Bright posters showed pictures of a calf with an extra pair of legs ludicrously misplaced at the front shoulders; there was the usual two-headed calf, shown eating placidly with both its heads, and the usual two-headed chickens; there was a colt with its hips placed immediately behind its shoulders and with no apparent trunk; there were several What-is-its, the most interesting of which was a mermaid which would turn out to be a hydrocephalic catfish.

Wayne had visited one of the stands one year and had found the freaks to be so much less interesting than their representations that he hardly took time to look at the pictures, now. It occurred to him that the place for which he was searching would be much more crowded in the afternoon and that there was plenty of time now for a visit to the various exhibition buildings, to see what was being given away in the nature of samples, badges, edibles, and advertising novelties. In the course of the next two hours he collected six or eight lapel pins, advertising various kinds of plows, cream separators and stock foods; a plain wooden cane on which was marked the proper depths at which to plant various kinds of grains; two blocks of rock-salt suitable for cattle; two cardboard fans; uncounted picture postcards; three samples of breakfast foods; a sample package of chewing-gum; a small lead cast of a tractor, and a number of other things of no more consequence.

At the end of Machinery Hall he could look down a gentle slope toward the entrance to the grounds and the Swine Pavilion. He now hurried to this latter, storing his new properties about him as he walked.

Blue Boy's new empire was a flattish building of unfinished brick. Two bas reliefs at the entrance represented what every new visitor at first took to be dirigible balloons. Closer examination disclosed that each balloon had a tail and a snout and that this was a not too subtle flattery of The Iowa Hog.

A strong odor of disinfectant filled the pavilion, for a spark of cholera in this pig Louvre might have flamed up into the destruction of thousands of dollars in irreplaceable lard. Wayne sniffed with distaste, regarded the dusty sunlight which came down from the high windows, and picked his way between the wire pens to Blue Boy's quarters.

All morning Blue Boy had been in a state of depression, for the entire character of his barn-lot had changed overnight. He remembered the exact corner where he had left his wallow, in the overhang of the barn, but he had visited the place a dozen times and there was not a handful of mud in the whole miserable world. True, there was a gurgle of water in one corner of this diminished estate, but when he put his foot in it his snout would not go in, so that it was hardly fit even for drinking.

Blue Boy blew glabrously and frowned. No need to speak of the coarse wire which had replaced the boards so necessary for scratching, or of the removal of the sun which delicately baked his belly each morning. All of these things were utterly intolerable, but they were not the worst. Ponderously and with low complaint Blue Boy ranged the wire pen once more. It was true—he was alone!

For a long time Blue Boy lay in the too-fresh litter of the cage, doubtfully awaiting his awakening from this nightmare, or the return of a Republican administration to nature. When Wayne arrived and touched his father's shoulder, however, Blue Boy's

77

position had completely changed. His hind legs were extended behind him like a pointer's; his tail, which he could move three quarters of an inch, was at the polar extremity of this range; his eyes were impatiently expectant.

The world might have said that he was reading the placard which set out "Class A, Poland China Breed Sows, ESMERALDA, Owner, Jacob Strait, Corydon, Iowa," but Esmeralda knew that he was not. For fifteen minutes she had been regarding him with that false wariness which is coquetry in every species; for fifteen minutes he had simply stood there. Blue Boy's coral snout, keener and more informed than any Casanova's eyes, which had brought him information that muliebrity was still abroad in the exploding universe, had also told him that it was abroad in the person of a Red-Headed Woman.

"What's the matter with that fool?" Abel asked his son. There was always more of engineering than romance in pig biology for Abel.

"I don't know. Gee, if he'll just hold it until the judges see him! How do the rest of them look, Dad?"

"Nothing to worry about yet." Every moment new trucks came up to the pavilion and new pens were occupied by complaining hogs. At each side of Blue Boy were males so obviously inferior that their owners spoke to Abel softly and humbly. Let them have their neat markings; Blue Boy was midnight polished into a blackness more colored than any color. Abel poked at the snout between the meshes.

"Go lie down and rest and get a little fat on them bones."

He turned to his son. "What have you been doing all morning?"

"Oh, just kind of walking around."

"I think I'll stay around here and see what kind of hogs show up. You go ahead and enjoy yourself. Blue Boy might feel homesick or something."

"All right, Dad." Wayne left the odor of disinfectant and the atmosphere of annoyance and started back up the hill.

The excitement of the Fair was over the whole grounds now and they could hear the buzz of the crowds that thronged the garish streets, and a chorus of barkers, faint and melancholy in the distance, below Campers' Hill. Wayne plunged into the Midway and began searching seriously for a particular hoop-la stand.

It was, though he did not know it, a minor mira-

cle that he found it. The particular carnival company which paid the Fair for the privilege of oper-
ating its various swindles on the Fair Grounds, had
happened to keep a few of its barkers for service at
Southern fairs and amusement parks throughout
the winter and had happened to send a particular
one of the barkers thus retained to this Fair for a
second time in the ensuing fall. Usually this was
not done, for identity is not a desirable thing in
such businesses.

It was the barker himself, who, counting on the
rusticity of the boy, actually found Wayne. He
hailed him from his stand.

"Hello, buddy! Bring down any bears with that
revolver?"

Wayne remembered the hateful voice, turned,
and faced his quarry. The barker was grinning
broadly and the crowd before the stand, a third of
it metropolitan, as Des Moines understands metro-
politanism, sensing fun, grinned with the barker.

Wayne turned fiery red. He was not used to so
much attention and he was extremely angry. Frake
common sense told him to say nothing, not to make
a fool of himself. He grinned back, almost naturally, and ambled up to the counter. On a terraced

stand were rows of plush-covered disks and on each of the disks was a prize. There were bottles of perfume, pearl necklaces, pen and pencil sets, ormolu clocks, safety-razors, and on two disks were pearl-handled revolvers. Hanging on a peg at the side were dozens of wooden hoops, exactly like round embroidery hoops.

Any of those hoops would go over any of the disks, for many customers, at a certain stage of annoyance, would insist on a verification of this hypothesis. With the hoop he kept in his hand, the barker could show that the hoops would not only go over, but would go over easily. Shrewdly pressed he could show that the hoop in the customer's hand would also go over, and it was not very noticeable that it went over a good deal more snugly.

Hitting a nail-head at ten feet with a BB shot would have been no more difficult than it was to ring the better prizes, but the proportions of the objects made the hoop-la test seem much simpler. If the hoop dropped perpendicularly it would settle down over the prize and the disk. If it had any important horizontal trajectory it would not. Scattered over the stand were a majority of prizes, completely worthless, which could be hooped by any one—badges, celluloid dolls, rings with glass jewels, and so on. To ring the more important prizes one needed at least as much special skill as is required to run off ten billiards regularly—this though there was no visible difference in the size of the disks.

These were things at which Wayne had guessed during the past year. Nevertheless, he sauntered up to the stand very confidently.

"Well, no hard feelings," said the barker, quickly, to forestall any remark which Wayne might be considering. "Here, have three rings on the house."

The boy accepted the rings quietly. Had his whole year's work been for nothing? He would soon see. He paused a moment to let the pulses of rage in his temples die down. Behind him people were laughing and advising on the prize he should try for first.

Quietly, without heeding them, he aimed for a disk on which an indubitable note for one dollar in United States currency reposed. The hoop spun, dropped and settled over the disk with the quick intimacy of one who has just found a long-lost and dearly beloved relative.

The barker stared. "Here, here," he said. "You're enjoying the courtesy of the management. Don't cost us money!" He replaced the dollar bill with a large tin and celluloid medal which said in red letters, laconically, "Out for a Good Time." They cost the company a dollar and a half a gross.

It worked! Then those long days in the carriage-house had been well spent. Wayne poised the ring in his hand and gave it an expert flip. Again the ring settled over the disk abruptly, with an air of having been put there by God.

The barker reluctantly handed the boy the second dollar. "Here," he said, "that ring's warped. Lemme give you a good one."

"It's all right," said Wayne, and hooped his third dollar.

"All right," said the barker, loudly, seeing his opportunity, "step up, ladies and gentlemen. You can all see how easy it is. Step right up. The prize you hoop is the prize you get. Three rings for a dime and prizes worth up to twenty dollars. You all seen this young man take three dollars off the board with ten cents' worth of rings. Who's next?"

"Give me three more." Wayne had no more chance of recognition than an honest Senator at a power trust investigation.

But public opinion suddenly came powerfully

to his assistance. The few observers who had been watching casually had now increased to a large crowd and none of them pushed forward to buy rings. All were intent upon Wayne and the barker.

"I don't think he's a capper," he heard some one say; "the barker's certainly trying to dodge him."

Anger flamed up again in Wayne. "I'll be the next, Mister," he said loudly. "Here's my dime."

The barker could not ignore this, with the attention of the crowd focused on the boy. "All right, buddy, here are your rings. Hope your luck holds out."

Wayne took the three rings and studied the board. "You didn't put back any dollar bills."

"Those were a special inducement," the barker said bitterly.

"I suppose those necklaces are fakes, too," Wayne replied, "but I'll take a chance on one of them for three cents." He flipped his ring and the barker handed him the necklace. In rapid succession he added a vanity-case and a clock to his prizes. The vanity-case was molded in a single piece of pot metal and the clock had no works. He tossed them on the ground.

With his next dime he hooped a bottle of bad

perfume, a pile of twenty-five sticks of chewing-gum and a pewter salt and pepper shaker.

"All right, fellow, you've had your fun," said the barker, who had lost about thirty-five cents on the second dime. "Now run along."

"No," Wayne said, "I want some more hoops." He put down a dime. The barker looked at the crowd, which had examined the vanity-case and the clock and was becoming more and more unfriendly, and tossed out the hoops. "See if the safety-razor's any good," some one urged. Languidly, the boy tossed a hoop over it. It, also, had been cast solidly in pot metal.

"See if the pens and pencils are any good," Wayne was urged. Certain of his virtuosity, the boy tossed the ring back-handed and watched it settle down over a pen and pencil set. The set consisted of a real pen and a real pencil of very inferior quality, but worth more than ten cents.

"Listen, kid," said the barker, "I want to talk to you." He muttered the words as he leaned over to hand Wayne his last acquisition.

There was a menace in his voice that alarmed the boy. "All right," he said, and stepped back into the crowd. With its spectacle ended and the barker gloomily silent the people soon drifted away, leaving only trails of stragglers who stared at the terraces of prizes contemptuously.

The barker's attack, after he had drawn Wayne over to the end of the stand, away from a few remaining observers, was oblique.

"You know what I'm paying the State Fair for this stand here?"

"I don't know."

"Well, it's more money than you'll ever see all your life. Now, to-day you've practically ruined this stand. You spent twenty cents and you took out three dollars in cash, and besides you made people think my prizes ain't no good."

"Well, they aren't," said Wayne.

"Listen, fellow," said the barker, moodily, "did you ever hear of intangibles? As long as nobody wins those prizes they're just as good as they look to be. Now you've come along and you toss them out where people can see them and criticize them. All their intangible value is gone. I pay a lot of money to work this place and you've practically ruined it. I could go to the State Fair board and I could have you put in jail for libel, criminal libel. That's twenty years maximum or three years minimum. How would you like to spend a little time in the federal penitentiary?"

Wayne laughed shortly and uttered an uncouth word. The barker veered. "Anyhow I could get you in a lot of trouble. The police are put here to protect us and all I'd have to do now is call one of them and you'd be put in jail—overnight, anyhow."

"Oh, would he?" The voice was spirited and feminine and came from behind Wayne's elbow. "Well, my father is an inspector of detectives and I say he wouldn't. I say you would."

Both Wayne and the barker stared. The girl was possibly seventeen, but her aplomb would have supplied a dozen women of forty. Very gamine, she could have been pretty in no other way. She had pulled a white béret down over curls which it was still evident were dark red; she had slipped a thin white sweater and a very short and tight skirt over curves which were precociously rounded; incredible lengths of net-hosed leg reached from the skirt's edge to the top of her high-heeled slippers.

"Say, chippy," said the barker, "how did you get into this?"

Wayne did not understand why the girl suddenly became very angry. "All right, if you think so," she said to the barker and turning her back to him, she suddenly began to examine the grounds. None of the Fair Police were near at the moment.

"Listen, sister, I didn't mean anything. I don't know who you are or where you come from. I was just having a private conversation with this lad here."

"I heard it. I saw the whole show. If you want to stay open after to-day you'll sell him all the hoops he wants."

The barker was suddenly very much on the defensive. "But I can't do that, sister. He'd spoil the whole thing. First place, I lose money on the prizes. Second place, nobody'll pitch while he's here—they watch him. Third place, he throws away the prizes and when people see them close they ain't so anxious to have them."

"You oughtn't to tell him such stuff, anyway. If he thinks police will throw innocent people in jail for the likes of you, he'll lose all his respect for the law." Suddenly her face lit with an idea. "Say, why don't you hire him for a capper?"

"As how?" Then he caught the notion and turned to the boy. "Say, buddy, instead of looting this place, how would you like to make some easy money?"

Monday Morning

Wayne hesitated. He still hated this man. "If it's honest."

"It's honest. All you got to do is just about what you did to-day. Every day about this time, if there's a crowd around here, you come down and stand around a minute. That'll give me a chance to get three dollar bills on the stands. Then you walk up and say, 'That looks easy!' and I sell you three rings. You ring the bills and you say, 'It *is* easy' and kind of walk away like it bored you. You can keep the bills for the trouble."

"And he caps your act for two dollars and ninety cents! Mister, there ought to be five of those bills and you give him his five dimes for the week's hoops now."

The barker looked at the girl with awe—"Lady, I'm glad your pa is a detective and not a burglar. There'll be five bills." He handed Wayne five dimes.

Wayne looked at the girl uncertainly. "You think it's all right?"

"What's the matter with it?"

Wayne looked uncomfortable. "You see, when I come up here last year I was trying to get a pearl-handled revolver. I spent just about all the money I had—eight dollars—and when I got the thing it was just a piece of solid metal with a couple of little strips of pearl on the sides. Even so, I wouldn't have minded it so much if he hadn't kidded me in front of the crowd. I didn't like that."

"What's that got to do with it?"

"I went home and fixed up a stand in the carriage-shed and got one of Mother's embroidery hoops and practised. I practised a little every evening after school and all the Saturdays it rained and Sundays. I figured I'd come back here and make as big a fool out of him as he'd made out of me. Now you want me to help him out."

"You practised all year for that!"

"Hard. I didn't show you anything." He reached over the counter and took a handful of rings. Suddenly—so suddenly that he seemed almost to have made a single gesture—they flew to all corners of the stand. Each nestled ·down on a disk. The barker gaped. The girl stared.

Then quietly the barker went to the cash drawer and drew out several bills. "Here's your eight dollars, buddy. I know when I'm licked. Our deal stands, if you want."

Wayne followed the girl away from the stand. "Gee," he said, "I don't know how to thank you."

He offered her the bills. "You sure are entitled to this, anyway."

She pushed the money away and looked at him thoughtfully. "I'll tell you, there's other hoop-la stands on this ground. If you wanted to come and win me a necklace or something—there's a pretty nice coral necklace on one of them that would go with my hair—" she smiled impishly and pulled off her béret, so that her head seemed suddenly to burn.

"Fine! Anything you want! It was a mighty good thing your father is a detective, wasn't it?"

The girl laughed warmly, intimately. "You didn't believe that! My father's a stock-show manager. He's helping with the shows over in the Stock Pavilion. I don't see much of him. You could get me an orangeade, too, if you wanted to."

They drank the cool and agreeable mixture of citric acid, synthetic flavoring, and sugar and went on up the hill to the hoop-la stand where Wayne won her a box of chocolate maraschinos, a coral necklace, a bottle of perfume, a real vanity-case, a leather purse, and other accessories as she pointed them out. With a ten-dollar bill the manager persuaded Wayne not to visit the stand any more during the current Fair and the boy began to feel fantastically wealthy.

Further exploitation of his gift had to be postponed until after lunch, however. He left Emily—they had soon exchanged names—agreeing to meet her at two o'clock under the grand stand, to watch the horse-races.

AFTERNOON

CHAPTER V

AFTERNOON

MELISSA FRAKE had already established her usual contacts with the families camped on each side of them for a hundred feet. The first two hours of conversation between good farm women is always the same—crop conditions. Once having settled their right to call themselves the worthy wives of good farmers, the women drifted off into recipes, clothes patterns, sewing, the church, the scandal about one preacher who had once administered the Methodist Episcopal see at So-and-so, and thus by easy stages to the lamentable condition of public morals—for instance, I know a woman—

Judging of the cooking exhibits, fancy sewing, oil and water-color paintings, pastels, pen, pencil and pen, and pencil art did not begin until Tuesday and so the wives of the camping farmers invariably dedicated Monday to "getting settled." The art exhibits were hold-overs from late Victorian days when a certain preciosity was expected of even mid-

dle-class farm wives who had attended public
schools; the exhibitions were now almost completely
preëmpted by country school-teachers who flour-
ished these accomplishments to their boards as extras
over and above the requirements of their curricula.

Abel Frake had spent the morning in inspecting
the entries which would compete with Blue Boy and
had already awarded his animal first prize. In fact,
others than Abel had done so and some in Abel's
hearing, so that he was in high good humor.

"Blue Boy's madder'n the old rip about something," Abel told his family. "I think maybe he
don't like the mash or something. If he'll just stay
mad there ain't a hog that ever was or ever will be
that can touch him. The madder he gets the purtier
he is."

Mrs. Frake was laying out the lunch on one of the
long wooden tables, freshly painted, which marked
the middle aisle of the tent grounds. Hard maples
and locusts shaded the tents and the tables and made
a pretty pattern on the cloth. Noonday quiet had
come on the Fair Grounds. All up and down the
hill, as far as they could see, farm wives were bringing kettles and jars out to their families.

"For what we are about to receive, Lord make us

truly thankful. Amen!" Abel prayed over the food, and added, uneasily, "I wonder if I ought to have brought some oats from home for Blue Boy. He's certainly acting funny—though he does eat."

"Oh, I think it's just the change, Dad."

"I suppose that's it." Abel helped himself to some cold boiled ham. "Believe they've got more stands than they had last year."

Wayne nodded at his acquisitions. "About the same. They've still got the butter statues of a girl and a calf, in an electric refrigerator, you know, and the freak shows are just the same. Souvenirs just about what they regularly run."

Abel looked at the prizes which Wayne had brought home, and laughed. "How'd you get that pile of trash? What did you have to pay for it?" Absently he opened a package of gum and abstracted two sticks.

Wayne hesitated. "Paid forty cents for it. I took it off a hoop-la stand." It would not hurt to tell them a little more of the truth. He need not mention Emily. "I practised some this summer with one of Mother's embroidery hoops. A fellow gave me five dollars if I wouldn't come around his stand any more this Fair."

Abel Frake laughed again. "What kids will think of! I guess that tin revolver got under your skin— eh?"

"I took most of this stuff off of him. I'm going to make him sick of swindling people." It was not the resounding and detailed story which he had intended to tell, but he was doubtful—or rather, he was not at all doubtful—of what his family would think of Emily. Underneath, he knew, she was a nice girl, even if she did dress a little funny. Her mother was dead—she hadn't had any mother to tell her that her dress concealed practically none of her seductive anatomy. She'd traveled with her father to horse-shows all her life, lived in hotels, been in the company of horsy men—no wonder her conversation was somewhat more sophisticated than one would have expected of a child of her years.

She was a pretty little thing, and she was going to get passes to the track, in the inclosure next to the paddock, from her father for both of them.

"Can I have this?" Margy pointed to the bottle of perfume.

"You and Mother can have all of that stuff, but you won't want the perfume. We—I tried it, and it smells like the stuff the barber puts on your hair."

"Oh, Buddy, you're nice!" Margy immediately began to make an allotment of the prizes for herself and her mother. Her mother was given all the more sedate items. "Will you take me down to the Midway and throw some rings for me this afternoon?"

"I guess I'll have time right after supper. I met a fellow I ran into here last year, this morning. He lives in Des Moines. He's going to get us passes to the amphitheater from a newspaper fellow he knows, on the Register." He was rather proud of that lie—it was detailed, explicitly and highly credible, and it would account for many odds and ends of his time.

"Oh, I wanted to go this afternoon. I'll have to wash dishes—"

"I'll take care of the dishes this evening," her mother assured her. "When you and Wayne get back we can all go to the pageant and the fireworks in the amphitheater together."

That meant that he would have to reserve one hoop-la stand for Margy, but he could explain the matter to Emily. "Sure," he said, "that sounds great."

He hurried off after lunch and was at the desig-

nated extrance ten minutes before Emily was due.
He was still there twenty-five minutes later when
a taxicab pulled up and let her out.

"I'm awfully sorry," she said. "I had to have some
money to bet on the races and Daddy had gone in to
get some fresh clothes. I had to go clear in to town
to the hotel to get hold of him. Come on, we'll miss
the first race and I've got a sure thing." She referred
to a list in her hand. "I don't know so much about
horses, but Daddy always gives me a list. He could
make a fortune on horses if he didn't have a weak-
ness for long shots. The reason long shots are long
shots is because they haven't got a chance—he knows
it, but he doesn't believe it yet."

"I've got some money."

"You keep it. Horse-racing is a bad game, unless
you know."

She approached an elderly man with a small square
despatch case swung from his shoulder on a strap.
"Three dollars on Tessie B. to win and five on Rolling Stone to place." The man gave her two slips
and took her money. There was sudden turmoil in
the inclosure. It seemed that several horses had
"scratched" and Wayne had a sudden ludicrous pic-

ture of dismayed horses being disqualified for rubbing itching noses with their front hoofs.

Emily seemed hardly to know that he was there. "Good! That means the five is safe, even if I lose the three."

A growl of impatience came from the crowded grand stand, and in the judges' stand, raised on ten-foot stilts above the track, an excited conference took place. The horses, pulling at their bits, reared and turned with the jockeys. Their silky flanks already showed dull patches of perspiration and their necks were arched and ridged with the hysteria which makes a race-horse a race-horse.

Wayne glanced up at the long grand stand, maggoty with people, and felt a momentary disgust. Far beyond the end of the stand he could see a Ferris Wheel, turning and pausing, and the wind brought down the reedy, far-away piping of "Take Me Out to the Ball Game." All about him were fat, red-faced men, wormishly alert, gamy to the eyes and to the nose, under the hot sun.

He was about to tell Emily how poor these creatures were in contrast with the strong, intense and eager animals tugging for the race, when he saw that

she was peering through the crowd, as intent upon
the dropping of the flag as any one of them. He
thought something so strange that he had to think
it again before he recognized it as his own—

"A fine little mare!"

There was a shot, a swift thunder of hoofs, and
the horses swept past the judges' stand.

A white barrier disappeared, a little farther down
the track, and Wayne suddenly realized that Emily
was surrounded by six-foot men who shut the track
completely from her sight.

"What number's ahead on the turn? Who's on the
rail?"

"If you'll put your arms down at your sides, I'll
hold you up by your elbows." The horses came clat-
tering past and a tremendous shrieking began in the
grand stand—"Tessie B., Tessie B." She was the
favorite. Emily, too, was screaming, "Tessie B." On
the last furlong Tessie B. was suddenly turned loose
to run and left the field three lengths behind, while
the grand stand and the inclosure went mad.

Emily shrieked, "Tessie B.," one final time and
then turned her head quietly to Wayne. "You can
put me down, now." She laughed at the blank expression on his face.

"That's why half of these people think they like horse-races," she explained. "It gives them a chance to jump up and down and yell, after sitting still and saying things in polite tones for a year. I like it, my-self. There's so many times I want to yell when it would get me thrown in the booby-hatch. I won eight dollars—three on my five-dollar bet and five on my three-dollar bet."

She made her bets for the second race and re-turned to him. "That's awfully nice of you to hold me up there, but I'm afraid I wore you out."

"I could hold you up there all afternoon. You don't weigh anything."

She gave him a comradely smile. "I'm afraid you'd get pretty tired of me about three o'clock. If you could just hold me up right at the start and when the horses get to the last turn, though, it would be lovely of you."

It was four thirty before the last race was over and the crowd began to pour from the amphi-theater.

"I'll bet you feel like a derrick they've just built a big bridge with," Emily said. "Come on and I'll buy you some hot dogs and some orangeade to build up your constitution. You're the real hero of the

103

day, but I've made a cleaning. Twenty-two dollars. If Dad had made twenty-two dollars every day he bet on the horses, we'd be rich now."

They sat down in a little sidewalk café and she pushed a five-dollar bill into his hand. "It looks better for the man to pay." She hushed his protest. "You've earned your hot dogs. Besides, you ought to know that if any lady ever attempts to pay for anything you ought to let her. It's a good habit to encourage."

She ate delicately but with appetite. The girl puzzled him more and more and some of his curiosity evidently showed upon his face.

"No," she said, smiling gently, "I'm not a wild woman and I'm not what you'd call a very tame one, either. My tendencies are good, but it's so much fun to do things you want to do, that don't hurt you or anybody, that I nearly always do them."

"I'm sorry," he was wise enough to say; "I've lived on a farm all my life and I've never seen anybody the least bit like you. But I was just thinking you were nice, and not—"

"No," she said, "you don't have to apologize. If you'd been thinking that I'd've slapped you." The half-serious mood fell from her and her eyes danced with mischief again. "Do you want to ruin some more hoop-la stands before you go to supper?"

"I'll tell you," he said uncomfortably, "my sister wants me to take her down and win some things for her, so I've got to save a hoop-la stand. Then the folks are all going to the grand stand to see the fireworks and they want me—" He stopped at the cold and bitter light which flickered for an instant in her eyes. Suddenly she burst into laughter.

"I never saw you in my life before this morning, and there's so much cat in me that I'm jealous as the devil on account of this girl. I should have known that any one like you would be here with some one. Of course, I can't monopolize your time. I do wish I could have kept you for my derrick, though. I don't suppose I'll see another race this week."

Wayne stared at her with bewilderment. Then he, too, laughed. "But it *is* my sister." For the first time since he had met the girl he felt that she was really the age she appeared—not thirty-five. "She really is my sister." He had a sudden access of honesty, but somewhat conditioned honesty. "There's a girl I go around with sometimes back home, but she's not at the Fair." For once he felt more sophisticated than Emily.

State Fair

The girl stared at him. Suddenly she reached out and gripped his hand as it lay palm down on the table. "You're a darling," she said, and rose to leave.

"Ten thirty at the hoop-la stand?"

She nodded. "To-morrow morning."

EVENING

CHAPTER VI

EVENING

It was a hell of a Fair, was the thought which was drifting around in Margy's mind and which would have shocked and offended her if she had heard it put into words. She had crept off quietly in the afternoon and eaten five cents' worth of cotton candy. Subsequently she had taken a ride on an utterly uninspiring giant swing. Then, with nothing much to do, she strayed off to the Exhibition Building, where she looked at pies without seeing them and wished that Harry were with her so that she could quarrel with him.

Her mother was carefully scraping the supper dishes, her father was talking with a man from the neighboring tent. The words "Hoover's a fathead" and "capitalistic tariff" warned her that there was nothing amusing in their conversation. "But not for a Catholic" did not even promise a good, hot religious argument—it merely meant Al Smith.

"Come on, Sis."

She put a dry plate carefully on the shelf, washed and dried her hands and took off her apron. Wayne was waiting for her at the entrance of the tent. He seized her hand good-naturedly and they ran down the hill together—he pulling on her arm and she making small shrieks. The shrieks were purely conventional—Wayne could have swung her off the ground and carried her, if he had wished, and she knew it; also the flutter of her skirts revealed strong, beautifully shaped legs, which could have taken her down the hill twice as rapidly, if necessary.

"Father!"

Mrs. Frake smiled and pointed to the children. Abel Frake pulled on his pipe and his eyes twinkled.

"They're certainly a fine pair," said the neighborman. "Mine are clear grown up and married," he added, wistfully.

"They're never clear grown up," Mrs. Frake assured him. "Just when you think they are—when you're about to realize that they think their own thoughts that are as good, or maybe better, than yours, but different, and live different lives, they do something like that that shows you the babies you knew are still inside them somewhere."

She turned to Abel. "Can you remember when

they used to run down to meet us coming from town Saturdays, that way?"

"You're getting old and sentimental," said Abel, gruffly. His gruffness was the tenderest part of a gentle character.

Mrs. Frake continued to watch them until they had disappeared among the lights and crowds of the Midway. "They'll be back pretty soon," she told her husband. "You'd better get ready to go to the show."

"A mighty fine pair o' animals," the neighbor added, before Abel could leave. "Give you two hundred dollars apiece for them, on the hoof, Abel."

Abel laughed. "You could buy a good pair of horses for that. Horses are better draught stock, but I think I'll keep my youngsters."

When the children returned, Margy had her arms full of prizes of all kinds and Wayne had ten dollars—the price of his promise not to return to the stand during the Fair.

The Frakes were all proud of each other. Their egoism was not personal; it was the agreeable, affectionate pride of people who are proud to belong with the persons who constitute their family. Mrs. Frake loved and admired her husband and her chil-

dren almost blindly; Mr. Frake had never told his
wife that he wondered if she would ever grow less
young and less beautiful; each of the children felt
that they were the offspring of unusual parents.
There was none of the tension in their farm life to
make them impatient with each other very frequently; there was a placidity and a kind of intel-
lectual self-containedness in it—the independence
of long hours at solitary labors—which had pre-
vented them from ever being bored with one another.

In four clanks they were through the turnstile
together and then they had passed up the concrete
ramp to the pop-corn-scented grand stand. A program boy looked at Wayne and Abel and avoided
stepping on the family's feet, but he called back
hoarsely, "Getcha pogram here—list of scenes and
cast of characters only ten cents! Getcha souvena
pogram here. Ten cents, a dime!"

"You want a program, M'lissa?"

"I'd rather just sit and see if I can make it out
watching it."

The lights of the grand stand suddenly dimmed
and were replaced by a brilliant glare in the field before them. A fat woman appeared and said things

which the loudspeaker system rendered pleasantly unintelligible. Somebody uttered a razzberry which was stilled as an usher approached. The spotlights sought out a platform behind the speaker's small dais and the Garden of Eden appeared.

The chantings of a choir brought to the stands what none of the Frakes recognized as part of "The Creation" and then Adam and Eve appeared in fig leaves somewhat smaller than bathrobes. Subsequent to the Garden of Eden, Jerusalem fell, Christ was born and perished on the cross, Columbus discovered America, Washington rashly crossed the Delaware, Lincoln freed the slaves and almost before the last spiritual of the blackened singers, kneeling with their broken chains before the Emancipator's—the Iowa Historical Museum still preserved souvenirs of his political cunning—feet had died out, Andrew Volstead rose in the House.

Beyond the stage dim figures scurried among the dog tents which were used for dressing rooms; dim lights burned in the stables where blasé grooms discussed to-morrow's possibilities; faintly, like a wash of surf, the momentarily attentuated noise of the Fair came up from behind the grand stand. The moon, who made the first gods and rules the rounds of men's lives and of women's, peeped sleepily and humorously into the back arches of the building. Volstead spoke eloquently but indistinguishably. By the very emphasis on the scene, however, it became apparent that Adam had delved and Eve spun, that Christ had suffered and died on the rood, that Columbus and Washington and Lincoln had lived and struggled and died in order to make it impossible for people to obtain the more agreeable mixtures of ethyl alcohol. Then the entire cast came out and sang "Iowa, My Iowa" to the tune of "Maryland, My Maryland" and two persons out of five in the audience thought, with a thrill of pride, "highest literacy rate in the Union!"

The pageant would have annoyed and mortified Christ, but it had elegant costuming, lavish lighting effects and fantastic scenery—the Frakes had found it quite entertaining.

The fat lady, who was the local president of the W.C.T.U. which was presenting the pageant, came out again and spoke valiantly into the rising tide of noise; retired unheard but unbowed. Mrs. Frake reached into a generously buttered—but what butter!—sack of pop-corn which Wayne had somehow managed to achieve during Volstead's long speech.

Evening

"I got every bit of it without a program," said Mrs. Frake.

"It seemed to wind up kind of flat," Abel said.

"Well, if we could of heard what that man said about the World War—but anyway you knew what he *would* say—"

Margy interrupted. "It wasn't the World War. It was something about prohibition. The W.C.T.U. is giving this."

"Well," said Mrs. Frake, maintaining herself in the right and Margy in the wrong with a phrase, "it was something important."

Afterward there was a display of fireworks—roses in red and green fire, the battle of Château-Thierry in complicated skyrockets and finally, of course, an American flag waving mildly in red, white, and blue fire. The band played "The Star-Spangled Banner" and the crowd, simple, great-lunged, and emotional, sang the banal song as well as it could, perhaps, be sung.

"Can Wayne take me one ride on the roller-coaster?" Margy asked as they were slowly working their way to an exit.

"I don't see why not," Mrs. Frake answered. "Don't you children stay out all hours, though."

"We won't!" Margy seized her brother's arm and they went up to where the roller-coaster roared at them like an iron animal with asthma.

"She's so pretty, it's a good thing she looks like you," a low voice murmured at Wayne's shoulder, but when he jerked around there was no one there. Margy looked up at her brother.

"What was that?"

"Nothing. Somebody who thought she knew me, I guess."

Then he saw a glimpse of red several yards away in the crowd. At the same time Margy let his arm loose and the crowd surged between them. When he looked back, his sister was gone.

Margy hunted for Wayne for a few moments, then she was convinced that it was useless to attempt to find him in the torrent of humanity which was still pouring from the amphitheater. "Darn!" She liked her brother; liked him as an escort. But she was not going to be defrauded of her roller-coaster ride. Perhaps he would be there when she got there. But Wayne, searching in the crowd for her, did not think for several moments of finding her at the roller-coaster.

Evening

In the meanwhile Margy had paid her fifteen cents and stood in line awaiting a car.

"All right, lady." There was one man in the car, a young man, who wearily waved a small card at the loader. Margy caught a glimpse of the card and recognized a miniature reproduction of a logotype she saw every day, the masthead of the Des Moines Evening Tribune. With awe she realized that she was about to occupy a car with the Press.

The Press was a young man of twenty-seven or eight, with sleepy eyes, a pleasant, not unattractive face, and a faint smile. His suit, of light gray tweed, set off a well-browned face and picked up hair of platinum blond for which any chorus-girl would have given her soul a dozen times over. He had evidently been around the world hundreds of times, had tired of wine, women, and song, and had taken up roller-coastering as an End in Life.

Margy took a seat demurely in the place to which the attendant beckoned her, at the young man's side. The bar was dropped over their laps and the car started, slowly.

Before they had gone twenty feet, Margy realized that she was not riding on the roller-coaster of the previous year. The first climb was tremendous, was mountainous. She felt a faint alarm. The young man lay back, relaxed, inspecting the Fair Grounds from the increasingly advantageous heights. He took out a cigarette, looked at it critically, and put it back in his pocket. Margy smiled and nodded at the cigarette. He thanked her with a glance, but shook his head.

The next moment they fell ninety feet.

The car brought up with a crash, literally leaped over a hump in the track and exploded around a curve which was banked almost perpendicularly. Frozen with terror, Margy half-rose against the rod which held her. Instantly the lazy smile on the young man's face vanished, his chin thrust forward and he grasped her arm and pulled her down. She caught only the word "fool" at the end of the remark which he addressed to her.

The car now went into a delirium of motion. It whipped around curves; it bounced and leaped over upgrades; it plunged wildly down sheer falls of fifty, sixty feet—occasionally it ran smoothly for a few rods to give Margy time to re-collect her fears. The young man looked at her curiously. Then abruptly he seized her about the shoulders, pulled her

118

over to him and buried her face in his coat lapel, which smelled pleasantly of lavender and tobacco smoke.

Without the slightest notion of what outrage this situation might portend, Margy felt a distinct sense of relief. The young man's arm held her firmly and she found that when she could not see what the car was doing, its antics seemed quite unalarming. They ran down a long, pleasant grade and came slowly to a stop.

Her knees trembled as he helped her out.

"Sorry to be so rough, lady, but I was afraid you were going to faint. You're white as a sheet, right now."

"I never fainted in my life," Margy said with dignity, and then she added with a weak smile, "but I might've, that time."

"Good girl!" the young man said with approval in his tone as well as his words. "You've got stuff. Want to try it again?"

"Not for anything! Not for anything in the world!"

"It's not nearly so bad the second time and the third time it's positively tame. You know what to expect. You can shut your eyes at the worst places."

"It's terrible!" But Margy looked at the car doubtfully and the fine inbred talent which women have for forgetting what happened the other time made her waver.

"Come on!" He waved his card at the attendant and the man held back a line of customers for them. "You can hide your face again if you get scared." She stepped into the car.

"You live in Des Moines? You look like one of the girls up at the University." Flattered out of attention to her environment, Margy started to shake her head, then merely gasped as the car gave its first dreadful swoop and spun around the curve.

"Baby, you'd make a soldier! You're the bravest thing I ever saw in skirts!" He shouted at her as she smiled up at him, rather painfully. Again he put his arm about her shoulders, so protectingly that she could not object. And she did find it rather a comfort.

"Listen, girl," he said, as they were rolling slowly in; "it was mean of me to get you to do that. I know you didn't like it, but I like you, and I'll buy you something to eat or drink. I just wanted to see what kind you were—most girls, you know, that are beautiful are usually a lot of silly idiots."

Evening

She was beautiful! She had always wondered if she were beautiful. Any looking-glass could tell her that she was pretty, but beautiful was something else, and better. His tone was so casual, so frank, that she could not find it in her heart to object. She looked at him sternly, however.

"Don't be that way! I'm no black-haired villain with mustaches. It's only that you're a nice kid, that I like. Come on and have a steak with me and a cup of coffee, and I'll take you to the bosom of your family and if we ever see each other again, it will only be because I've run you down and had a proper introduction. My name, by the way, is Pat Gilbert. Yours is—let me see—Helen—Helen—no—Margaret—ah, yes—Margaret—"

"Margharita—Frake. How did you know?"

"It's a vaudeville trick—an easy one. You say, 'Mary—no—Anne—no—Mildred—no—!' When you get something close to the right sound their faces change and then you go along on a line of names with that sound. When you hit the right one, it's no trouble to tell, like I did now. You can see whether they're English-American or German-American or what they are. You're English, with some German. I'd have guessed Rose next, then

Elizabeth and Anne after that. That would have put me close to about every common English and German name. Then if I didn't hit it in a name or two, I'd have asked what it was."

"And it usually works?"

He laughed. "No, I've only tried it on people I've met regularly before—that is, run into at some friend's house. Mostly men. Here we are."

He ordered a steak, specifying the exact length, breadth, thickness, and manner of cooking. "And if it's not," he concluded, "I'll just pay for it, I won't eat it."

"Mister, we'll try," said the waiter, simply.

Margy would not allow the steak order to be duplicated. She ordered a crab-meat cocktail and cold consommé, both strange dishes. She was not hungry and she intended to be educated if she could not be nourished.

"But if you're a newspaper man," she asked, "what were you doing on a roller-coaster?"

"I like roller-coasters," he said simply.

"You like roller-coasters!"

"I like to ride on them. There's motion, there's excitement, there are a dozen stimuli. Maybe it's psychopathic. Everything that any one does any more outside of a recognized, drab pattern is psychopathic. But I get a lot out of roller-coasters."

He flashed a curious, angular grin at her. "Why were you on the roller-coaster?"

"I like to ride on roller-coasters. If they're not too fast."

He shrugged his shoulders. "There you are. You're an intelligent girl—you're almost as old for a woman as I am for a man—women learn everything sooner —but you like to ride on roller-coasters. So do I. As soon as we finish, let's go back and ride on that one."

Although his speech was sober, his expression was roguish. He had the face of a boy, about to put a tack in the seat of some one he liked and respected. Good fun was its own excuse.

Margy laughed. "Idiot! All right, I will."

Their orders came. Pat ate hungrily. Margy, to her astonishment, found that she liked both of the things which she had ordered very much. Usually, things which she didn't know about and ordered were pretty bad.

"Where are you really from, pretty girl?"

123

"Brunswick. That's close to Pittsville. Pittsville's thirty-five miles from Ottumwa and fifty miles from Keokuk, almost on a line."

"Brunswick! Do you know the Storekeeper!"

"Of course. How do you know about him?"

"I had to get a story in Mt. Zion once—somebody killed himself and the way it started it looked like a swell mystery. I got back to Brunswick running the thing down and talked to the fellow in the store. He was grand. I almost missed my train. He was full of Shakspere, Dickens, and Mark Twain. There was a traveling-man in there, a young fellow from Wisconsin U—full of Kant and Hegel and all that.

"The Storekeeper didn't know anything about Kant and Hegel—any more than Jesus knew about Confucius and Buddha—but he knew his own notions. That's a great man—at the bottom—stuck in that little country store."

Pat's acquaintance with the Storekeeper moved him to a completely new position in Margy's categories. She was the least bit overborne with Kant and Hegel and All That, but the fact remained that Pat knew and respected the Storekeeper and was blood and bone like herself—not some strange and incomprehensible growth.

Evening

Pat gurgled with pleasure. "Second time I ever saw him was a bright sunshiny afternoon. He was taking the chains off his car to go over to Pittsville. I said, 'Good Lord, man, it hasn't rained around here for a week! Don't you take your car out Sundays?' He said, 'I just put these chains on this morning.' I said, 'But it didn't look like rain then.' You know what he said?"

"What did he say?" Margy, who knew very well why the Storekeeper put chains on his car on certain sunshiny days, asked Pat curiously. She wanted to experience his delight in telling her.

"He said, 'I figure if you put your chains on, days you're going somewhere, it will be so much trouble putting them on and taking them off that They won't have it rain.'"

"That would've been Wednesday afternoon," Margy said. "He always goes to the bank Wednesday —that's understood. Saturday's his busy day, so we shop as much as we can weekday mornings to take some of the load off Saturdays. Weekday afternoons nobody bothers him because then he's always reading Dickens or the financial pages. Sometimes he goes to sleep and you can't get what you want."

"They play horseshoes out in front of the store.

The Storekeeper's got all the corners of the horse-shoes filed so that you can't get cut with them, or cut your finger on them."

"He thinks everything always happens for the worst," she said.

The man sat up with excitement. "Yes! He's right! Follow down any happening of your life to the extreme limit and you'll find that the final results don't please you. Did you make the best grades in a class in school? You lost friends, the people who expected to make the best grades. Did you find that some one you liked liked you too? Your dearest friend hates you. Did you make a dollar that you never expected? The things that you bought with it only brought you discontent. You can't beat it. That's why there were hermits—"

"Hermits" Margy knew as a kind of cookie. She suddenly felt drowsy.

"I've got to get home. The folks don't know where I am."

"I'll take you home. But say, you were going with me once more on the roller-coaster! It'll only take five minutes."

She asked him a question.

"Yes. I work for the Register."

"We get that paper every day. Do you ever have your name in it?"

"Almost every day; also its evening edition, the Tribune, sometimes. Don't you ever look for by-lines?"

"What's a by-line?"

"That's the name of the man that the story is by, printed over the story. You look for my by-line." He tossed a bill to the waiter and rose. "Come on. This is your third time on the track. You'll enjoy this."

"Just once. I'm awfully late for home."

"Where do you live?"

"We're up in Tent City, just beyond the little gulch."

"I can get you there in no time."

She was prepared for him now, in whatever wily manner he should attack her, but she was not prepared for the circumstance that he did not attack her at all. They rode around the roller-coaster and he did not even put his arm about her shoulders. She found the sensation comparatively mild.

"You see?" he said. "It doesn't amount to any-

thing. It's just the surprise the first time."
They strolled out to the sidewalk. "Well, good
night."

"No, I'll see you home."

"Oh, I can get home all right—oh, all right."

THE THIRD DAY

CHAPTER VII

THE THIRD DAY

THE day was hot, but it was dry heat and in the shade the perspiration had little opportunity to collect. A slow, steady breeze blew across the State Fair grounds, bearing odors of pop-corn, cattle, oranges, dying grass, and humanity. Curiously enough, the blend was not unpleasant.

Wayne rose, threw on his clothes, and hurried to the bath-house. The cold water spurted down upon him and he delighted in the sensation on his skin. He rubbed himself vigorously with soap, held up his armpits and exposed his loins to the shower to wash off the last spots of lather, and chafed himself down with a rough towel. He liked the play of muscle upon his breast as he drew the towel up, and for a moment he sparred with Jack Dempsey. He toyed with the deadly dark-skinned fighter a few blows and then he brought a decisive left-uppercut up from the floor.

Dempsey went down like a felled ox. "Felled ox"

was the flattest a man could go down. Oxen are inelastic, essentially, and the way he hit them, thought
"Fighter" Frake, they would all be inelastic after
the first bounce following a swing of his powerful
left—or right, or whatever he should use.

Naturally, Emily was in the first row to applaud
him. Oh, you've whipped the greatest fighter of all
time! Emily, I've never smoked, or drunk, or dis-
sipated. She would appreciate the delicacy of "dis-
sipated." But neither has he! No, Emily, but you
can't beat Frake stock. Muscle is different in the
Frake stock—feel here! Great Heaven, your stomach is like steel plate and I can feel the play of sin-
ews under your chest like fine steel rods. We're like
steel, Emily, you're right. Like steel, physically and
emotionally. Ah, Wayne, but not to me! Well—

"Listen, kid, are you ever going to get out of that
shower?"

"Mister, if you don't like it, there's a great big
river less than two miles from here. You can wash
there or drown there—and it's about as easy to
drown as it is to wash, for some people."

Wayne knew that the man had chosen him because under the high-cut door he could see that his
ankles were slender and white. The man outside

could not see that above the point where the door cut off the view, they swelled up powerfully into more than six feet of man. There was a rumble of laughter from the other booths.

"All right, kid, you've got to come out of there sometime."

And what if the man should be one of the hard-faced railroad men he had seen in Eldon, or one of the more obvious thugs he had seen about the grounds of the State Fair?

A Dempsey-fighting Frake could not flinch. Wayne sneered, a tentative sneer, unfolded his shoulders like a stretched fan and threw the door suddenly open. He confronted a short, fat man, whose belly rolled down over its own heels—an obvious bully, and an even more obvious coward. The vicious and angry face slowly changed. It grew more moderate, but it remained vicious. Finally, it smiled, sickeningly.

"All through, friend?"

"I'm all through," Wayne said, coldly. "Were you asking me before?"

"No," said the fat man, "I just got here this moment—there was a fellow went into one of the other booths—"

"All right," said Wayne. "If you were the other fellow, you'd get a hell of a good thrashing."

"But what's all this? I come in to take a bath and—"

Wayne trotted up the path toward the camp in his trousers and bathrobe. He had dared chance and chance had been kind to him—perhaps even a bit too kind to him. It was already nine o'clock. He'd better get his breakfast and get about his business. As he came up the hill, Margy came smiling toward him. How she'd changed in a day!

"What became of you, Wayne?"

"I looked all over for you, Sis. What'd you do?"

"Oh, I looked everywhere, and when I saw I'd never find you I went down on the roller-coaster and took a ride."

"How was the roller-coaster?"

"It's a lot better than last year. It's higher and faster. I rode it a lot of times before I came home."

"I looked all over for you. Then I went to the roller-coaster, but there were a lot of people getting on. I knew it would just be luck if I found you, so I came on home and went to sleep."

"You didn't care what might happen to me?"

"I thought you'd have sense enough to see to getting home all right. We all went to bed—and you don't look especially murdered."

"Don't be silly, Wayne. I wasn't murdered. Don't you think I can take care of myself?"

"Of course, I do. That's why I came home." His tone was disappointingly matter-of-fact. She could have teased him more, but suddenly she decided that she would not. A moment later they came to the breakfast-table.

"To-morrow," Abel said solemnly, "they judge Blue Boy."

"Dad," said Wayne, "what do you think?"

Abel looked at his son confidently and kindly. "Don't worry, Wayne. The beast will win. I've talked to people all around the Stock Pavilion and they say nobody's ever seen such a hog in all the years they've been here."

"Do you think he'll win, Abel? Do you really think he'll win?"

They all looked at Mrs. Frake. It was evident that her desire that Blue Boy should win reached out beyond their own simple impulses. "I've been to the State Fair all these years, but I've never seen many of the family entries win a sweepstake. You really do think he will win, don't you, Abel? You're not pretending?"

Abel chuckled. "I know why you want Blue Boy to win, Melissa. You think if Blue Boy wins I'll be fairly fit to live with for a whole year. I can just promise you right now, I won't. If Blue Boy wins sweepstakes, I'm going to start out on horses. I ain't ever going to be satisfied with what I get. I'm going into other things I can't get—you can count on that."

Melissa Frake looked a long way beyond the breakfast-table. Then she smiled at Abel. "It would be pretty tiresome listening to you talk about when Blue Boy won his sweepstakes for the next fifty years, Abel."

He kissed her on the cheek, fondly. "Don't worry, Melissa."

He looked up at the children. "What'd you two do all day yesterday? What are you planning for to-day? Coming down to-morrow to see Blue Boy win?"

Wayne spoke first. "Of course, we are, Dad. Don't you think we're interested in Blue Boy? We'll be out there, don't you worry."

The Third Day

Abel patted his son on the shoulder. "I know you're interested. It's just a contest, of course, like running a furlong, or seeing who can roll a peanut the fastest with his nose. There's no difference at the bottom as far as patience and practice and work is concerned. But one reason I want to win is that all of you have understood the patience and work it's taken to bring up a critter like Blue Boy. Well, to-morrow's the day."

Mrs. Frake spoke timidly. "Do you know whether they judge the pickles to-day—does anybody know whether to-day's the day for pickles? I've got Blue Boy and pickles all mixed up."

"Let's see the program, Mama."

After a long study, Wayne managed to find the class and hall under which pickles were entered. He spoke excitedly. "But they do judge the pickles to-day, in the Exhibition Building. It's at two o'clock they start—you'd be Class A, wouldn't you, Mama? —that's the class they start on. People that've won prizes before."

"Which hall?"

"It's the Main Hall—right after you go in the door. All you have to do is go up to the Exhibition Building and go in either entrance. If you go in the south end you just walk up to the other end. At two o'clock the judges begin tasting the things and looking them over. I suppose it'll be pretty well finished up by four o'clock."

Mrs. Frake sighed. "That's a long time when you're waiting anxious. Will you be there, Wayne? Margy?"

"Sure, Mother," and Margy added, after her brother, "I'll be there."

It was obvious that Abel would have to be near his hog, so that Melissa did not even ask her husband if he would be present.

A little later Wayne announced that he was going down to see what was going on around the Fair. His sister looked at him curiously. Wayne, she decided by his nonchalance, was Up to Something. Then, with a little thrill of pleasure, she remembered that she was Up to Something herself, so she said nothing.

Emily wore a straw hat of light gray, a gray sweater and skirt, and a yellow scarf. She smiled with pleasure when she saw Wayne's admiring glance. "Less conspicuous," she explained. "I didn't realize that if your folks should see us they'd especially—notice red."

The Third Day

"They'd like you," Wayne said with enthusiasm, if not conviction. "Why can't I take you up for lunch to-day? All I'd have to do is tell Mother there's another one coming."

"No, Wayne. I don't think we'd better plan that —for a while, anyway."

They wandered down to the little stand where the third round of the horseshoe-pitching contests was in progress. There was real pitching now, not the kind which Wayne had seen the first day. It was not a question of pitching "ringers," for every contender could do that on almost every pitch. It was a question of putting the steel bows on the stakes so that they could not be knocked off and so that "toppers" pitched by the opponents would bound off their uncompromising metal surfaces. Taken up to a definite level of skill the game had again become almost purely a game of chance.

"That's good pitching," said Wayne.

The girl looked at him with amusement. "You ought to be good at that the way you pitch hoop-la rings."

"I am, but not near good enough for fellows like those."

"But it's all the same idea."

"No, the horseshoes are heavier. You have to do that with your arm—it's altogether different, like punching the bag or playing the piano."

They wandered on. "You going to bet on the races again this afternoon?"

"Are you planning something?"

"You see, my mother has some pickles entered at Exhibition Hall. She's got a lot of prizes for cakes and so on. I thought I ought to be there to see if she wins a ribbon."

"I think you ought, too. Maybe you'll see me this evening. Anyway, I stole two tickets out of Father's vest this morning. They're playing 'Blossom Time' at the Princess to-morrow night—it's a Broadway company, Howard Marsh and everybody. I thought you might like to go."

"Stole them! But if he was going to take you—" He stared at her. There was a moment's silence. She glanced at him whimsically. "Dad wasn't going to take me."

"Oh!" He was silent again for a moment. Then he said eagerly, "But sure, I'd love to see a show in Des Moines. I've never been to one. Why do you say maybe I'll see you this evening?"

"If you see me, that will be all. To-night's horse-show evening. The first horse-show evening Dad will want me in the judges' box with him, out in the middle of the ring"—she grimaced—"to add to the decorations. It might be worth while to come," she added demurely. "Miss Iowa's going to be there with Daddy."

"I'll bet nobody will notice her, if you're there."

"My, my! Did you say you'd lived on a farm all your life? I guess it's a good thing." Then she said seriously, "I probably won't see you again till to-morrow evening. I've got to go over my clothes to-morrow morning, and I'll find so much mending to do it'll take me all afternoon. You come to the Fort Des Moines Hotel and ask for me. We'll eat there on Daddy's bill and then go to the theater. Tell your folks you'll be out late, because it's a long show."

"But—" he protested.

"If I see you to-night I'll wave at you—when Daddy isn't looking. Good-by, Wayne." She disappeared as they reached the foot of Campers' Hill and he went up to his lunch.

MARGY

CHAPTER VIII

MARGY

PAT was more than a block away, in the crowd, when Margy first saw him. There was something gallant, debonair, about the carriage of that shining head, bare to the sun, that picked him out even in the jostling mob of the Midway. And he saw her, too, for he threw his arm above his head stiffly, in a kind of vertical Roman salute, and even at that distance she could see him smile.

A few moments later he stood beside her on the steps of the roller-coaster entrance. He looked at her face for what seemed a long time.

"It was dark when I saw you before," he explained, as she turned her head half away. "At least, it was electric lights."

"I suppose," Margy said, "it's not very nice of me to really meet you here—but I like you. Only, don't keep saying things like that."

"Don't you like them?"

"Of course I like them—and I don't like them. They sound good—but they aren't honest. You make me feel wickeder when you say them. I know you mean them, in a kind of a way, but I know you oughtn't to say them."

Pat roared. "I'm in my place—you've put me there. Come on, let's ride the roller-coaster."

She caught his coat sleeve timidly. "I didn't want to be mean about it. You know what I was thinking, don't you?"

His face was serious, but somehow more alarmingly tender than his words had been. He spoke soberly. "Margy, I know what you mean. You're a lovely, sensible girl. Don't think I'll ever make any mistake about that. I'm not a cheap flirt or a drug-store cowboy or anything of the sort. When I first saw you last night I thought you were awfully pretty—that's why I held your head. Afterward, I thought you were brave—I admired you—and you could be friendly and candid.

"You've probably got a boy somewhere back home; I've got a girl in Fredonia, Missouri—but she's going to be married in September, dammit—and so let's see the State Fair together and then forget about it. Life's complicated enough—at least,

for women—without picking up lifelong friend-
ships on every roller-coaster car."

"All right, Pat, if that's understood."

"Understood. Come on, get in."

To her surprise she found that the precipices of
the preceding evening were merely mildly exhilar-
ating. She was so obviously nonchalant about the
terrors of the ride that Pat did not even have an
excuse to put his arm about her shoulders.

After the second trip, she stirred as the car came
in and Pat turned to her solicitously.

"Want to go again?"

"No." She looked up into his face—she was tall
for a girl, but he was taller—and smiled with faint
irony. "It's too tame."

"There's a better one out at Riverview Park—
that's the city's so-called amusement park—but it
takes practically weeks to get out there from here."

"They ought to have collapsible roller-coasters—
like collapsible drinking-cups—that you could pull
out longer when you got used to them."

"Gee, I wish we were in New York. There's a
little park across the river there where the big drop
is two hundred feet. There's a good one at Coney
Island, but this one beats them all. The Kansas City

roller-coaster is tame and the one in St. Louis is terrible." His eyes grew dreamier than a stamp collector's. "There's a pretty fair one outside Los Angeles in a little place, and a wild one in an amusement park outside Chicago. The one in Philadelphia is nothing and in New Orleans they don't go in for them. That one in New York is the best one I ever rode on. I'm not kidding, with all I know about roller-coasters, I thought twice before I went back on it."

"You've been everywhere?"

He chuckled. " 'Seen everything and done everything.' No, I haven't. When I first started in at this racket I went on the bum—work a little in this shop and a little in that shop—and circumnavigated the country. That business is finished for newspaper men —Billy Hearst and his likes, may the tribe decrease, have got us coming in like sewer diggers now, at nine o'clock, and digging sewers. I've never been further outside the country than a glimpse of Mexico and two weeks in Montreal. All on the same continent. But I had six months on the old World in New York—best paper there ever was. What you can't see in New York you can't see anywhere.

Margy

It's God's greatest gift to mankind, except for the dirt, Tammany, Dagoes, and subways."

They had drifted toward the Engineering Building when Margy suddenly came out from under the spell of almost unintelligible songs of Araby.

"Pat! I've got to get up to Exhibition Hall!"

He looked at her blankly. "What's the matter?"

"My Mother's pickles are being judged right now."

"What!"

"My Mother's pickles. They're being judged."

He seemed dazed. "Well, they can't give them more than thirty days unless they've been guilty of a felony."

"No, idiot. They're going to see if they can tell that they're the best pickles in the world, or whether they don't know pickles. I ought to be there this very minute."

"Oh, I see." He spoke seriously and regretfully. "You know I've been covering the feature angles of this place for three years now, regularly, and I've never been inside that place. Maybe there's some good features there. Come on, let's get up there."

She hesitated.

"What's the matter?"

"I'll have an awful time explaining—if you come with me—"

The regret in her tone was so evident that he did not tease her. "When do you think they'll have all those pickles sentenced?"

"Around four." She looked up hopefully. "We could meet each other somewhere then."

"Meet, my eye. I'm going to shadow you. You don't know me. I don't have the slightest idea in the world who you are. But you'll see me around—don't give yourself away."

"Oh, Pat! But I might give myself away!"

"Well, that'll be your fault. You can't keep me from going where I want to. I've got my duty to remember. Right now I think my duty is to go to the pickle hall and get a feature story about Mrs. Frake's prize-winning pickles. Swell head—'Pickle Pickers Pick a Peppy Pickle'—don't try to say it. If they win the prize, that's that. And if they don't I'll write a story, 'It is unfortunate that a lot of Iowa State College Yahoos with boiler-plate where their palates ought to be, overlooked the magnificent, statuesque pickles of Mrs.—Mrs.—'"

"A. R. Frake."

Margy

" 'A. R. Frake of Brunswick. Apparently these judges were accustomed only to tea tasting—and not good grades of tea. Mrs. Frake's pickles were far and away the most memorable specimens of marinating that have ever been pranced out from their stalls before a cheering public.' "

She laughed. "You idiot! You couldn't get a thing like that in the papers. Not actually."

He regarded her solemnly. "If your mother loses, those identical words will appear in the Des Moines Tribune. I run a column on the Fair. I can say what I please. Anyway, about pickles."

"But you've never seen the pickles."

"I've seen you."

"Oh!" she pouted, smiling.

His face was filled with mock concern. "My God, what have I said? Too impulsive, Gilbert, you're always too impulsive. I was thinking of nice, little, tender, delicious, shapely, sweet pickles—"

She giggled, charmingly. "That's enough. It was a slip, but I know what you really think of me.—Pat, that story wouldn't be fair."

"Why wouldn't it? Aren't your mother's pickles the best?"

"Yes, but the judges—"

"As far as I'm concerned, you're the Erasmus of all pickle judges in the world. I couldn't say less."

They had come almost to the door of Exhibition Hall. "I'll see you afterwards, Pat?"

"Unless you suddenly have a touch of total blindness."

Exhibition Hall, with its dozens of booths, its long promenade running around a central tier of stands, was jammed when they reached it. Pat had already disappeared, but Margy was very conscious of every step she took and every gesture that she made. The audience was largely female and all were watching the peregrinations of two women and a man who moved solemnly along the tables and opened the jars, taking out bits of the pickles displayed and tasting them.

There seemed to be millions of jars. Occasionally a judge would make a note on a small tab which he carried. The foremost woman took a slice of cucumber out of a jar, put it in her mouth and stopped. She lifted her eyebrows at the other judges, pointed at the jar and nodded.

Margy stared at the jar. If that was not the way her mother had packed her pickles there was something wrong. She counted the layers. Twelve! Green tomato, cucumber, onion—no one but the Frakes had ever known the formula for that old pickle, inherited and improved for four generations, ever since tomatoes had ceased to be "poisonous." Bay leaf, mace, clove, a stick of cinnamon, chives, Cayenne, a faint touch of tarragon, and the least suggestion of garlic—the Storekeeper had always had an awful battle with the Keokuk jobbers to get the things that Mrs. Frake demanded.

"That's sure for a ribbon," a woman beside Margy whispered. "She's Dean of the Department of Home Economics at Ames. Whose is it?"

The women about her craned. "It looks the least bit like mine."

Margy saw her mother, only a few feet from her, and pushed through the crowd. "Mama! That woman looked a long time at your pickles—"

"Probably thought they were so bad she wondered how anybody would have the nerve to send them here," said Melissa Frake, mendaciously. "Anyway, I'm not so sure they were mine." She was calm, if a little breathless. "Where did you come from?"

"I was right over there." There were only forty or fifty men in the whole room, but suddenly she saw Pat, talking with one of the judges who had stepped into the audience. Pat spoke heatedly; the judge laughed and nodded. The business went on for a long time, for they were judging all of the cookery exhibits. Finally the judges retired, and when they returned they were armed with their schedules and loaded with blue, red, and yellow ribbons. A herald followed them.

"First prize for beaten biscuits: Mrs. Sylvia Lewis, Rural Route Two, What Cheer, Iowa; Second Prize, Mrs. Mary Bennett, Adair, Iowa; Third Prize, Mrs. Ruth How, Montezuma, Iowa.

"First prize for pastry: Mrs. Ada Duffield, Keosauqua, Iowa; Second Prize, Mrs. Eleanor Rowley, Cantril, Iowa; Third Prize, Mrs. Alice Short, Kilbourne, Iowa."

He went through a long list of comestibles of various kinds. In the raised breads department, Mrs. Constance Bridges Jones of Seymour seemed to be predominant; in the fried-cake division, Mrs. Dorothy Liberton from Story County was queen.

The judges continued to fix ribbons to exhibits until Margy could hardly endure it. "Oh, I wish they'd get to pickles," said Mrs. Frake.

But it was a long time later before they got to pickles and both Margy and her mother were tired.

Margy

"Pickles and preserves!" Both of them came to attention. "Sweet pickles, Mrs. A. R. Frake, Brunswick, Iowa, first; blahblahblahblah. Sour pickles, Mrs. A. R. Frake, Brunswick, first; blahblahblahblahblah. Pickles, unclassified, spiced pickles of Mrs. A. R. Frake, Brunswick, win blue ribbon and plaque for best pickle or preserve in department." The announcer paused.

Margy, who had been gripping her mother's hand tightly and more tightly as the announcement continued, looked up into the placid face.

"Mother, did you hear the same thing I did?"

"Yes, Margharita." Her mother sighed. "In a way, I'm sorry. I knew those pickles would have to win, and I almost didn't enter the spiced pickles on that account."

"But Mother! The spiced pickles won the plaque!"

Her mother shrugged young and rounded shoulders, slowly. "But what can I enter now? I've got the very most that woman can get out of the Fair exhibits. I've always come to the Fair looking for new prizes, better prizes. Now, unless I start raising horses or something there's nothing more to do." Suddenly, she smiled at her daughter. "I'm just joking. The Fair's enough fun even if you didn't have anything entered."

"Yes, Mama, but I thought you'd be pleased—"

Melissa looked down kindly at her daughter. "Margy, I'm so pleased that if I even pretended to let on to myself how pleased I am I'd probably have hysterics right here."

Margy laughed. "The plaque'll look nice in the kitchen."

Melissa stared at the crowds which were moving up and down the walk and sighed. "If Blue Boy will only win the hog judgings now, it'll be all any one could possibly ask of a State Fair."

They strolled back toward Campers' Hill together quietly, until suddenly a raucous voice broke the murmuring calm of the afternoon. "Stand still a minute, will you, lady? Both of you stand still. I want to take your pictures for the Register."

"What? Why do you want to take our pictures?"

The hard-faced little cameraman seemed amazed. Margy caught a flash of light gray toward her right. "Why do I want to? I'm a newspaper photographer, and if the Des Moines Register doesn't carry a picture of the best cook that ever lived, to-morrow, we might all just as well be dead."

Margy

Without going into the matter further, Mrs.
Frake posed. "Wish you had a jar of pickles," the
photographer said, "but this is going to be an ex-
clusive, any way you look at it. Just smile the way
you did, will you? Oh, that's fine! Put your hand
on your hip to hold up your dress a little—no!—I've
got to get a little cheesecake in this picture!"

"Cheesecake," said Margy. "What's that?"

"Don't be stupid. It's display of the female figure.
It's just a word us cameramen use. Meaning something it's always a soft job to photograph—well,
anyway—stand quiet—there's one—two—three—
Thanks!"

Thoroughly bewildered, Margy's mother asked
her daughter, "What was the matter with that
man?"

"He was just taking our pictures." Was Pat as
near as he had said he would be? "He wanted to get
your picture for the paper. It's mighty extraordinary for the same woman to win the prizes you've
won to-day."

"I'm going up and sit in the tent. I'll get my
plaque and so on to-morrow when I'm more settled.
I never realized what a strain it was to get something you wanted the worst kind of a way."

Intricate thoughts ran through Margy's mind. "All right, Mama. I'll leave you at the bottom of Campers' Hill. Mama, if I'd take a notion to eat somewhere on the grounds and go down to the grand stand by myself, don't wait supper on me, will you?"

"You mean you're going to eat somewhere else this evening?"

Margy pouted. "I haven't seen any of the Fair, except last night. I thought maybe Bud and I could go around—"

"But if you don't come up to the tent, Bud'll never find you."

"No, I just mean that we could run loose a little and see things, together or apart. We oughtn't to be tied down, Fair Week. To-night I'd just like to run out and ride roller-coasters and things, and see what's to be seen of the Fair, as I find it."

Melissa smiled at her daughter. "That's the way I was when I was young. All right—but come in a decent hour."

The girl caught herself so that she said, "Thank you, Mama" in some reasonable tone.

It was almost five o'clock when her mother walked up Campers' Hill. As soon as Margy was alone, some one at her elbow said, "Isn't that fine? She won all the prizes. And she had her picture taken!"

The girl turned quickly. "Pat, you devil! I knew when that photographer ran us down that there was something funny about the business. What did you say to those judges?"

He looked at her earnestly. "I didn't say a thing. There's nothing you could do with those judges. I said the pickles were running too much to form— do pickles run to form?—and that I'd like to see something unusual and good win once in a while, instead of a lot of Iowa State College recipes every year." He did not add that he had told the Home Economics director that his aunt, a Mrs. Frake, had some delicious pickles entered, but that with her well-known delicacy of taste and sense for the exotic—upon which the Register had frequently commented—the director would be able to discover them without even looking at the label. "I figured that if they judged on the merits, instead of on what credits they thought the Home Economics departments of their schools would get, that your mother would probably put up good enough pickles to win."

"You didn't have anything to do with the photographer, of course?"

"Oh, yes," he said. "I thought it would be a good picture scoop. I told him to be sure and catch you. D'you think he got a good shot?"

"He made us stand around enough. Pat—"

"What's this?"

"I told Mama I wasn't coming in for supper. I told her I wanted to look around at things. Do you suppose we could eat together somewhere?"

He caught his breath. "Margy—of course we could." They walked along the boardwalk, shoulder to shoulder. He held her arm firmly. His hand was warm, but she could not tell whether she resented his grip more than she liked it. She moved her arm away. He did not object. "Here. This is the best place to eat."

They went in to the little sidewalk restaurant and ordered their dinners. Both were silent, preoccupied. It was the first meal she had ever eaten away from her family.

When they had finished it was only sunset. The show in the amphitheater would not start for more than an hour. They turned to each other at once,

160

and each seeing the words that the other was about to say, laughed. They rose without a word.

From the heights of the roller-coaster, for the first time she had the opportunity to see from a high place the night burgeoning of the carnival. They rode and rode again, and as their car swept up to the peaks of the track each time, she saw the flashing into life of new banks of lights, seeming to burn up like some intricate fireworks, filling up the great picture, the gaudy booths, the gemmed buildings, the bright amphitheater, in what seemed a planned succession. A coronet of light shot around the octagonal edge of the Exhibition Building, and the Fair Grounds had formally entered the evening.

They rode, and in ten minutes, or fifteen minutes at the most, in the thin edge of the twilight, the whole appearance and character of the grounds were changed. Sections of lights on the outside fences blazed up successively, walking widdershins against the place where the sun had vanished. The basic green and brown of grounds and tents, with their little artificial glamour, swiftly glowed—romance was in the glowing, and delicious mystery in the shadows.

They said nothing; they watched. Away to the west the city suddenly threw up an answering luminescence—a response. The track dipped and turned and periodically it lifted them to watch this metamorphosis of the day Fair to the night Fair.

When all the lights were on, she sighed. The car slid down passively to its starting place.

They stepped out. "Like it?"

She drew a long breath. "Yes."

"It's time to get over to the amphitheater, I'm afraid."

His card took them down to a special railed box where were gathered a number of young men and younger girls, intent upon the crowd about them and busily engaged in making disparaging remarks about everything. "Hello, Pat." Two or three of them grinned and waved.

"This is the Press Section. All of these people have seen this, but they come out to make dirty cracks about it. That's Boyce of the Register, and Mamie Foster, the sob sister on the Tribune. The rest of them are bums from all over the two shops. You see, Mrs. Carmichael, the local president of the W.C.T.U., is responsible for the pageant. They give it alternate nights—the vaudeville fills up the other

162

evenings. Do they hate Mrs. Carmichael! Nosy, nasty, vociferous old swine! Sic semper W.C.T.U. So they turn out every pageant evening and give it a pan, just for their own satisfaction. The vaudeville to-night is a good show. They pan it just to keep in practice."

The display opened with a thunder of fireworks, the grand stand lights dimmed and the flood-lights at the edge of the track suddenly burned high. A streak of brilliance about a platform flashed on and men and women in white tights appeared upon the stage. Almost instantly they were tossing each other about, whirling across the canvas in backward and forward somersaults, pitching each other across the stage—the platform was filled with gutta-percha people who bounded in every conceivable fashion. A brass band materialized unexpectedly before the stage and the air was filled with music.

Stage-hands, slipping quietly in and out, threw up two long perpendicular bars behind the acrobats, and a line of silver shot between them. The acrobats vanished and a clown appeared. Several times he attempted to speak, waving his hands energetically, but his conversation was limited by the fact that he was able to utter only "Oof" and "Aak."

At last he gave it all up and climbed the ladder to the silver thread which ran across from two tiny platforms on the uprights. There he waited and shivered, while the audience roared with naïve and honest delight, until an apparition in shimmering, spangled tights rushed suddenly up the ladder beside him and sprang out, gleaming, upon the rope.

The apparition danced for a moment, then crossed to the other platform. The clown stood on his platform and trembled visibly. The crowd encouraged him, but for a long time he would not risk the crossing. Finally he took two or three steps, and immediately dropped to his hands and knees upon the high rope, and began to crawl. Balancing painfully, he advanced a few yards, and then the delighted jeers of the audience brought him to his feet again.

For an instant he stood proudly upright, then he fell off the rope, arms spread, feet flying. The crowd groaned. His chin caught and with a thrust of his arms he was upright upon the rope once more. There was a gasp and a roar of laughter. The clown began inching his way along the rope. He fell off frequently, now, sometimes catching by an arm,

164

sometimes by a leg, but that was expected. Then, a few feet from the farther platform and safety, an access of fright overcame him and he ran backward to the first platform. The crowd shrieked with laughter.

After the tight rope had been taken down—long after—there was a tank, and spangled mermaids dived from incredible heights. A quartet sang, there was a dancer, more acrobats, and fireworks.

She shook her head and sighed. They were waiting for the first press of people to get out of the amphitheater before they started toward the exits. It was a warm, though not oppressively warm, September evening, and they did not feel like fighting themselves out.

"What's the matter, Margy?"

"Oh, you wouldn't understand. That was so much fun—after the good supper we had, and sitting there with you—and now there's nothing to look forward to—the best is over."

"But, Margy, dear, we can do it again, to-morrow evening."

"But that would be just the same and I'd know it was going to finish up just the same. There's a first time for everything and you never can get it just the same, ever after. I remember when Dad brought back some ice-cream from Pittsville—"

They had reached the foot of Campers' Hill, and he guided her as they talked. "You know Schopenhauer says we live all our lives in pain—the pain of wanting something—and when we relieve some pain we think that that's enjoyment, when it's really just relief. You talk as if you believed that. I think you're a pessimist."

They sat down in a place which was screened, by two trees and the terraces of the earth, from all the world. They could hear faintly from the boardwalk across the ravine the occasional rattle of hurrying or strolling feet. The moon was low and the shadows covered them securely. From the farther reaches of the ravine came occasional shouts and laughter, and sometimes, for a moment a shrill voice.

She suddenly recognized, with alarm, that they were hidden. Her tent was not a furlong from them, but it might have been a hundred miles. But his first remark was so commonplace and so simple that it seemed silly to move or protest.

"I phoned the office from the grand stand.

They're going to use one of the pictures on page two."

"Mama will be thrilled to death. It's awfully nice of you to do that, Pat. You don't know what it means."

"Oh, I have an idea. Are you cold? You're shivering."

"The air's damp. I ought to go up to the tent and go to bed."

His hand fell upon her arm, gently, but with a hint of restraint. "The air's not damp. You're not cold. We're talking like fools about nothing we're thinking about. Do you want me to stop your shivering? Or whether you do or not—"

He suddenly caught her face between his hands and kissed her. She jumped to her feet. "What do you think I am? You can't do that to me! You said we were going to be friends and then you act—like a—beast."

"Sit down," he said quietly, and as she hesitated he caught her about the knees and brought her down, her eyes toward the rift in the trees and the stars. "I'm going to be your friend." There was something harsh and violent in his voice which terrified and fascinated her. "You've been wanting it for a long time, and you didn't know what it was. Do you love me?"

She was surprised to hear her own voice say, "I love you."

Horrible—horrible! She could not speak, she could not move.

"Ah, God," she cried, in anguish and delight.

BLUE BOY

CHAPTER IX

BLUE BOY

"Wake up," his father said. "To-day's the day they pick out Blue Boy for the finest boar was ever raised. Everybody out!"

He heard his mother rise quickly in the next cubicle. Then he heard his sister cry, out of broken sleep, "No—no—oh, I'm still half-asleep!"

He made some definite swishes and thuds which would indicate that he was dressing in all haste. Then he lay down quietly and allowed his eyes to droop half-shut. His father's pallet was rumpled and mussed—to-day was the day they judged Blue Boy.

Had it been an accident that Emily had touched her fingers to her lips before she waved at him last night? If he had only had opera-glasses! She had worn some kind of a shimmering white dress which made her look like a wheat stalk across the sun. But he could not see her face, half across the auditorium from him. She had lifted her arm, when she saw him,

171

and when she waved she—or did she? Certainly she waved.

"Wayne! You're going to be late for breakfast!"

"All right, Mother."

The bath-house was a hundred yards away. He jerked on the minimum essentials of clothing and rushed out of the tent at a sprint. He liked the showers. He wished that they had showers at home. Quickly he shaved, arranged his clothing and walked back up the hill.

Miss Iowa was a silly-looking fool. Any girl who would go in for that sort of thing must be pretty dumb and pretty cheap. She'd been brought out and introduced like an unusual heifer, or a prize sow. Next week, Emily's father had announced, Miss Iowa was to compete for the title of Miss America in Atlantic City. Champion human sow of America! But she'd never get it—they raised them better for that purpose in California. Rot! It was filthy to think about.

He spat on the grass and strode in to the breakfast-table. The whole family was waiting. His father, at the head of the table, was in the act of loading his plate with poached eggs and bacon, cut thick.

"Well, Wayne, you finally got up."

"I couldn't have been much behind Margy. I saw
her coming back from the ladies' baths just as I came
out of the bath door."

His father laughed, but with a high pitch in his
laughter. "No harm done. Come on, gobble this up.
To-day's Blue Boy's big day."

"What time is the judging?"

"The animals will be shown to-night. But they
ought to put the ribbons on the crates around four
o'clock. Those judges have sized the animals up
pretty well, right now. Once I know Blue Boy's
taken sweepstakes, I don't care whether they parade
him in a Prince Albert or a pink kimono to-night.
I don't care about watching his triumphal progress."

"Maybe we could all go down together—around
three thirty," Mrs. Frake suggested.

"I'd have to be down earlier than that," said Abel,
"but if all of you will wait around Blue Boy's crate
for me when you come in, I'll find you and we'll
look over the show."

"What do you children plan to do?"

Margy waited for her brother to speak. "I didn't
plan anything till evening," Wayne said. "My friend
in Des Moines got a pair of tickets for a show called
'Blossom Time.' I thought I'd go with him."

"That won't be over till late," Mrs. Frake said, thoughtfully. "Were you going to come back out to the grounds to-night?"

"Oh, sure—anyway, I suppose I will. He didn't say anything—" Wayne paused, confused, and wondered why he had said that.

"Well," Mrs. Frake smiled kindly, "we won't wait up for you. If you come in late, try to come in quiet."

"What are you going to do, Margy?"

The girl answered indifferently. "I'll go down with you folks to see Blue Boy get his prize. If Wayne's going in to town, I guess I'll go and see the moving-picture show this evening, and maybe ride once on the roller-coaster afterwards—maybe twice."

"I'm glad you can amuse yourselves," said Mrs. Frake. "I've just been running around so that I'm all tired out. I'm going to bed early this evening and get a good long sleep. The heat, and the people and the excitement and winning the prizes and so on kind of wore me out. And I've got lots to do to-morrow. I met that Mrs. Whittaker from Sac County at the contest yesterday and she and her husband are coming over to eat supper to-morrow evening. Then I've got to look up some folks I met last year on the steps of the Administration Building. I'd told them I'd find them there again this year and I've been so busy I haven't been near the place."

Abel put his arms around her shoulders and laughed. "Mama, every year you plan to come to the Fair all year, and then when you get here, as soon as you get settled and get the sewing and the washing off your hands, you begin serving company meals to all the hungry people in the State of Iowa. Now I want you to quit it and make Margy and Wayne do all the work, and go out and see a State Fair once."

"Abel Frake, I've planned and managed every one of our Fair trips, and never once has anything gone wrong—except maybe a cup or two—and every one has had a perfectly lovely time; me, most of all." She smiled good-naturedly. "If your hog was where my pickles are, you wouldn't be so bossy all of a sudden." It was a worn family joke that Abel and Melissa should accuse each other by innuendo of unsteadiness, irritability, and Napoleonic complexes.

"Where were you last night?" Wayne asked his sister, suddenly. "I heard you come in."

There was a crash of china and a silence. "Oh, my Lord," said Margy. "Do you have to shriek at a person, Wayne? Oh, I'm sorry—I didn't mean to be cross. It's so hot my fingers were wet."

"It isn't one of the set," said Mrs. Frake. "Now, Margy, you remember the argument we had about planning things? That might just as easy have been one of the set. Why wasn't it? Because, I said to myself, 'There's two things you've got to watch out for to save your china: company, because you don't know anything about them, and Margy.' Women know how to handle china and so they get careless. Men are awkward, so they're safe. That, Margy, is why I saw to it you weren't drinking out of the one from the set."

Margy giggled, and there was an almost hysterical note in her voice. "I'm sorry, Mother. I was thinking about something else."

"Say," said Abel, "I'm not going to be cheated out of my last word, and that was, that if my hog was where those three judges put your pickles, there'd be three of the awfulest bellyaches in this town to-day was ever seen or known of in the State of Iowa—but I wouldn't have any chance for a prize."

Blue Boy

Wayne wandered down to the grounds after breakfast and roamed disconsolately from stand to stand. He tried his luck on a wheel of fortune and after spending forty cents found himself in possession· of a kewpie doll. It was a rather silly kewpie doll, but it was not as silly as he was when he carried it. He tried lugging it nonchalantly by the legs but immediately discovered that despite its elaborate lace dress it wore no underwear. He right-ended it and wished to God that Emily were there.

The roller-coaster was rather good the first time, but very dull after that. By and by noon came and after lunch he read a newspaper in front of the tent and waited for three o'clock. The three of them started for the Stock Pavilion a few minutes after that hour.

The Stock Pavilion consisted of a great central auditorium with six wings running out from it at equal intervals. The hogs had been housed in the Swine Building and horses had held the Stock Pavilion until this afternoon, but the development of two new strains in the State had given hogs a special importance on this year's programs, and for one day they were given the larger building.

Abel's family found him near Blue Boy's crate

in warm but genial argument with the owner of an immense red beast.

"Smoked right, I admit," said Abel. "You take Virginia ham, that's famous, but it's made from measly razorbacks we wouldn't tolerate in this part of the country. If you want to spend more than a critter is worth curing him and dressing him up, you'll get a pretty good piece of meat, no matter what. You give a Hampshire shoat the same opportunities an ornery piece of Virginia razorback gets and you'd have manna—yes, sir, just manna. As for me, there's no ham I like so well as Pella ham."

"Smithfield—" said the owner of the red animal.

"When you buy a piece of Smithfield—which I never do," said Abel, "what are you buying? You're buying fifty cents' worth of curing and ten cents' worth of moral and physical ruin the way it's worked up by the scrawny hogs of Virginia. They don't raise any hogs in Virginia. A hog's got temperament. In Iowa, he's unhappy. Anywhere else he's miserable. Iowa'll always raise better hogs than any State in the Union. Hello, folks!"

Winning his argument by this simple device of recognizing his family, Abel smiled and shook hands with the owner of the red boar and moved up toward Blue Boy.

That animal was still standing looking as much like the Apollo Belvedere as his species would permit. What he lacked in contour he partially made up in intensity, in eagerness. Adaptable, intuitive, Esmeralda had long before decided that Nature was for the moment fundamentally and unfavorably disordered. She was not altogether certain whether Blue Boy was a hog or an illusion. She had lain down to sleep out the depression.

Blue Boy for four days had grown rapidly more conscious that he was a hog. Each morning he spent an observant ten minutes in touring his cage; then he took up his post with his snout against the wires, pointed at Esmeralda. The powerful hind hocks which would one day ornament a jar filled with white vinegar and bay leaf, touch the floor only with a foremost crescent. Blue Boy was great enough to assume this attitude; he was too great to change it.

"But, Dad," cried Margy, with excitement, "Blue Boy's already won! See, they've pinned a blue ribbon on his cage!"

"That's just the class award," Abel said with an

indifference which was betrayed by the trembling of his voice. "Best Hampshire boar. They're looking 'em over now to find the most physically perfect boar—all classes, sweepstakes winner. Ought to come pretty soon now. They don't have near so many entries to judge."

"Where are the judges?"

"They're in the next wing. There's a pretty good animal—no, here they come."

The judges paused at a crate up the line. They discussed a black-and-white animal with considerable animation, taking plentiful notes. Then they bore down directly on Blue Boy. All three of the judges, department heads from Nebraska U. and the State College at Ames, smiled at Margy and Mrs. Frake.

"Don't worry, ladies," a goateed man who might have been an etcher, apologized to Mrs. Frake. "We won't keep you waiting much longer." Then they looked at Blue Boy from all angles, moving around and around the cage and checking up on each other's notes in low voices. Blue Boy was bored, disdainful and annoyed. One of the judges reached into the pen and scratched the boar's back. Blue Boy voiced his resentment in no unmistakable, though rather indolent, terms.

Blue Boy

"Poise," said the judge, and laughed.

Blue Boy looked at the judge closely and then shifted his glance significantly to the cage opposite. "Ahoonk," he suggested, with relative mildness. "Ahoonk!"

The judge scratched him again and his attitude became even more tense.

They checked once more on Blue Boy's printed record and then moved off to the crate of the red hog.

"Aren't they going to give it to him?" asked Margy, in a repressed tone, when the judges were quite out of earshot.

"Of course they're going to give it to him. But they have to look at all the rest—just as a matter of form." Abel was nervous. Blue Boy uttered an asthmatic wish for his mud-hole and his mistresses.

Blue Boy allowed his heels to touch the pen floor. Slowly the approximate conviction to which Esmeralda had attained forty-eight hours before was forcing itself upon Blue Boy's masculine mind. He submerged the repressions of four days in the one philosophic consolation left to him. After all, it was quiet here for hours at a time, sometimes. Blue Boy considered sleep.

The judges passed on, comparing notes.

And they did look at all the rest. At four thirty o'clock, when the family was at a breaking tension and Abel had become almost ill-natured, the judges returned to Blue Boy's crate and chalked "1" in a large figure on the corner of the crate.

"Most remarkable boar I've seen in twelve years of judging and thirty-five years with hogs," said the Nebraska dean. The others congratulated Abel and added their assurances that Blue Boy was an unparalleled animal.

"Hardly ever you see an animal so well-developed that's got the spirit he has," said the Ames man. "I like to see a boar up on his toes, full of vitality."

Quite by accident, Esmeralda lifted the lid of one eye and looked at the judges. She could not smell her owner, so she gave one speculative glance at Blue Boy and went to sleep again. Blue Boy went back to the corner of his cage where the water gurgled, and lay down. The judges shook hands with Abel once more.

When they had gone, "Oh, my Lord," said Abel. "I own the finest hog that ever was, and the Storekeeper owes me five dollars."

WAYNE

CHAPTER X

WAYNE

ABEL and Melissa, with Margy, were to attend the show in the evening at the Stock Pavilion, and see Abel presented with the great trophy which testified that he had aided the State of Iowa by improving its hogs. Wayne was truly sorry that he could not be there and his regret was evident in his voice.

"Dad, I didn't have any notion it would be like this! They've never even given a trophy before—and they didn't haul the winners around the way they're doing this year. If I'd known I never would have told this fellow I'd go to the show. The greatest hog raiser there ever was and his own son not there to see him win," he lamented.

Abel was touched by his son's extravagant sincerity. "Son, you go on to your show. You can see that hog all you want to all winter and you can see me all winter, and the trophy. But you can't see that show but once. I didn't know about this myself till yesterday, and even then I wasn't sure.—

If it's anybody's fault you aren't there, it's mine, and it isn't anybody's." His voice lowered confidentially. "Son, I know how much this means to you —you go to the show and don't worry."

At seven o'clock Wayne entered the crawling street-car which rattled westward through East Des Moines, over the river, to the larger city on the west bank. It was cool when the street-car moved, and the lights and voices along the city streets filled him with a sense of mystery. Behind each voice there was a soul, no less wistful, no less curious about its own desires than his own. He looked at the people's faces, but they seemed alien, some held by this emotion, some by that, but all faint and sickly overcast. Suddenly he realized that the deep wants, the hungers of his heart were not reflected in his own face —that his own features indicated only some content and a little curiosity.

The lights were only dusk lights, but they hinted at the night to come. After a long time the car passed the two beautiful State buildings of Iowa— the Capitol and the Historical Building. A State with a history of less than one hundred years had already begun to look back at its past, like an intelligent child, hoarding what was good, exulting over what had once been bad. And so the car rolled down Capitol Hill and turned, crossed a stately bridge over the dark, shining water and ran a few blocks, jerkily, through the busy streets of Des Moines' Times Square.

He had worn his white flannel trousers and a blue serge coat, hoping that this was the dress for the theater. In Des Moines, it was as good as any. The clerk spoke to him respectfully and in a moment he was lifted to the tenth floor. He rang a bell.

"Wayne! Oh, but you look so nice—!"

"Emily!" A dress of frothy green silver swept the floor. Her hair, freshly waved, swept up from the proudly amorous face. A circle of jade about her throat suggested a lower barrier—which he promptly overleaped—for his eyes. An abbreviated jacket of ermine threw its petals up around her cheeks.

She smiled with pleasure. "I don't look like an urchin now? You like me? Oh, I hoped you'd like it."

He caught his breath. "I don't know how to say —Emily! You shouldn't have done this! How can I go with you like this! Anywhere you go people will see that you're the loveliest girl that ever lived. And

187

what am I doing with you in my terrible old flannels and my blue coat—I don't care, they're the clothes I ought to wear, they're plenty good for me. But a king would feel—out of place with you."

She was really moved. She led him in to the soft, rich little room. Suddenly she swung open a closet door, lined with a long mirror. "Wayne! Look at yourself!"

He saw a boy with a proud, gentle face; hair that curled darkly back; eyes that were not afraid to look at anything at all, a strong throat, wide shoulders, the thin belly and solid legs of an athlete. Reassured, he drew himself up gallantly.

"You're beautiful," he said simply, and took her arm.

The show was beyond anything he could remember ever having seen. The hero was splendid, so kind, so honest, so understanding; the heroine he accused only of a little stupidity; the music moved him to the bottom of his being. Once or twice he was near tears, and then he found himself suddenly in the midst of boisterous laughter.

He glanced at Emily doubtfully, but his emotions were her own. She was really very young, when she laughed, and when she regretted the sentence of death which God had pronounced on Schubert. The tears streamed down her face when he sang, ". . . and the glory of love!"

She clasped his hand. But the next moment the comedian was working his way in and out of incredible difficulties and both of them were convulsed. Surely, this was the greatest play that was ever written. Shakspere and his Hamlets—oh, all right, but not to be compared with this. And the play, whose whole success rested on notes written generations before by a poor, godlike, diseased German, came to an end.

It was only four blocks from the theater to her hotel. He took her to the door and there he would have turned and gone home—home to his tent on the Fair Grounds.

Suddenly she was his comrade again. "But you must come up. I've got a surprise for you. Just for a few minutes."

They went through the lobby together, and took an elevator. In a moment she had turned the key and they were in the softly lighted room. She ran over to the dresser, opened a drawer and took out a bottle which was half full of a glowing amber fluid.

"In big towns," she explained, "people always have a drink or two after the show to kind of get on their feet again. I tell you that thing upset me, and you, Wayne Frake of the Frake-Frakes, you were upset, too. You'd have been crying in the aisle if they hadn't brought in the comedian just when they did. I swiped this off Dad last night and I've got a bottle of seltzer and some ice."

Sin thrilled through and through him. "Are you sure it's all right?" Then candor caught him up. "Emily, I've never tasted a drop of liquor in my life. If you give me a drink of that, it's on your own responsibility. I don't know what in the world it will do to me."

She laughed kindly, and the spell of the moment caught her, too. "I've never drunk enough of the stuff to know what it's all about, either. But this is only half a pint and I'm sure it won't make us go out to fight cops, or kick Salvation Army tambourines."

"All right," he said, "if you want to take a chance, I will."

She made two drinks. They sipped them slowly. "It's kind of nice and warm in your stomach, isn't it?" she asked.

"I like it," he said briefly. Then he looked at her soberly. "How long does this stuff stay on your breath?"

She laughed. "When you wake up to-morrow morning, nobody will be able to tell whether you've been drinking liquor or eating oranges. I'll give you a lot of orange peel before you go."

They drank the rest of the whisky. He felt a gentle geniality stealing into his brain, but he felt nothing remarkably out of the way. His body was able to take up the little drug he had given it and dispose of it without any pyrotechnics. She looked at him steadily and soberly. A thought struck him. "Emily! But what if your father should come here?"

"He won't come here to-night. He's out on—he's out with a woman. And if he did come, he wouldn't come to my room. He wouldn't dare to. I'm supposed to be asleep."

He suddenly felt that the room was warm. The alcohol that he had drunk, running through his body, had made him perspire. "It's hot, isn't it? It was hot in the theater."

"Yes. Why don't you take off your coat?"

He took off his coat and felt relief. They were

quiet for a moment or two. "That's beautiful on you, Emily. I didn't suppose anybody could be so lovely—I ought to be getting back to the grounds."

"Not for a minute," she said. "Not till I fix you some orange peel. Oh, damn! This dress is like bearskin! I'm going to take off some of the tightest parts of it."

"Wait—" she said, and disappeared into the bathroom. He hummed, "Thou art my song of love . . . and the glory of love."

She returned, a kimono about her. "When you first knew me, you thought I was what you thought I was because I had a short skirt. And to-night you thought something else because I wore a two hundred dollar gown. Well, what do you really think of me?"

There was nothing under the lovely kimono but the lovelier Emily. He had somehow known that there would not be—!

FRIDAY EVENING: MARGY

CHAPTER XI

FRIDAY EVENING: MARGY

EVEN on Friday the glory of Blue Boy's triumph had not died out. The horse-show had come, and was going that night, but the grandeur that was Blue Boy, somehow, picked up by the Des Moines Register and the Tribune, had lingered over every stock section of the Fair.

For some reason, Blue Boy had been built up by the two papers to the stature of a Middle Western hero. Did you think of Governor Drake, of Tama Jim Wilson, of doddering Senator Allison, or Gullible Cummins, of Lillian Russell and Senator Copper King Clark—you thought also of Blue Boy. And Iowa's littérateurs—Rupert Hughes, Lewis Worthington Smith, Herbert Quick, Emerson Hough, Susan Glaspell, Ellis Parker Butler—why, was not this last author's greatest achievement called "Pigs is Pigs"?

Abel wondered a little, even in the greatest glow of his triumph, at the sudden fame which had come to Blue Boy. Even in Chicago papers they had shown the boar's picture with the caption, "The World's Greatest Hog." That hardly seemed reasonable, though Abel knew that the fact was a fact. Still, he saw no good reason why the country should be stirred by prospects of cheaper pork. Sport was sport, but pigs, it was true, were pigs.

Still, the adulation increased his pleasure in the award. He had expected the Register to be interested in the story, but he had not anticipated two news and four feature articles on the surpassing quality of Iowa breeding. Nevertheless, he did not object to them. The fact was that he enjoyed them, and he considered sometimes, "Maybe I'm underestimating the honor of owning the greatest hog that ever was. Maybe they're right." But after reading the stories, considering that a hog was only a bit of putty which one shaped by careful selection and breeding into whatever forms one desired, he decided that they might be right as newspaper men, in search of stories, but that they needed a breeder's point of view on hogs.

The end of the Fair was near. Already that hung over them, and breakfast had not been as cheerful as on the day before.

Friday Evening: Margy

"Well," said Melissa, "when it's all over, we've only got fifty-one weeks to wait until the next one."

Wayne came out of his tent and yawned. Melissa laughed at him. "Your friend ought to start charging you board. This is the second night you've spent at his house. I'll bet you boys don't get a wink of sleep. I'll bet you don't get home till all hours and when you do you fool around and never get to bed. I know how boys are."

Wayne yawned again. "He wants me to come over again to-night and go down to the University where he goes next year and see the gymnasium. He knows the watchman. He wants me to come up there next year—but I don't think it would do much good. Though I think I'll take a look at the place. It might be worth seeing."

Melissa Frake looked faintly troubled. "Why haven't you ever brought him over here? I'd like to meet your friends, Wayne."

"It's just one thing and another. He's awfully busy." He smiled at his mother confidentially. "It's only one more night. To-morrow night we'll be packing up to go back to Brunswick. I'd kind of like to spend this last night over there."

Melissa looked at her husband. She would have given Margy permission without consulting Abel, but Wayne was a boy, hence under Abel's final jurisdiction. "Do you see any reason why he shouldn't, Abel?"

"Oh, no. It's only one more evening and I think the more acquaintances you make while you're young, the better for you."

Margy spoke firmly. "Well, if Wayne's going to run all over the place, I'm going to go around the Fair and see what's happening. I've hardly seen any of it but the roller-coaster. So don't expect me home until awfully, awfully late. I'm going to ride the giant swing, the merry-go-round, and everything. After all, to-morrow night's the end of it."

"What are you going to do, Abel?"

Abel yawned. "You know, I'm just going to sit around here and maybe talk to anybody that comes in, but I'm not going to try anything much. The fact is, after five days of it, I'm just about tired out. I'm going to bed with the chickens."

"I'm going to bed just about the same time," said Mrs. Frake. "I always enjoy Fair Week so much it wears me out. Anyway, I want to get everything washed up and kind of cleaned up to get ready for to-morrow." She yawned slightly. "To-morrow we got to all pitch in and pack."

"This is a good day to rest," Abel corroborated placidly. "To-morrow we've got to pack and we won't be home till Sunday. Sunday evening, if I'm not mistaken, the younger members of our household will have people to see. And Monday"—he sighed—"back to the clover, the feeding of hogs, and the fence-post holes. Well, all good things must come to an end."

He rose from the table. Since Blue Boy had won the highest honor to which any hog could aspire, Abel's had been a difficult life. True, he could drop around to the building in which the swine were kept and see people admiring his hog, but this was no longer a very exciting experience. Blue Boy had already established himself as the greatest of all hogs and compliments seemed hollow after that great compliment.

For the most part, Abel amused himself by talking and arguing with his neighbors. He loved to argue, for he usually won. He was armed with a shrewd, practical, trenchant point of view which almost invariably won him his decision in pitched dispute. None of these people could think as the Storekeeper could think, or argue as the Storekeeper could argue, but it was interesting to get all kinds of angles on things.

The children disappeared after breakfast, and again after lunch, with a precipitancy at which Mrs. Frake smiled. She had come to the Fair when she was young—younger—herself. She finished the luncheon dishes and turned to a pile of sewing which rather startled her. It was curious how things got torn and worn and buttons pulled off during Fair Week.

Abel returned from his argument, sat down in a steamer chair, stretched out and yawned. Mrs. Frake glanced across her mending at him. Her needle peered in and out of a button, looking now at this side, now at that, like a monkey with a mirror. Suddenly the needle paused.

"Abel! You're going to sleep!"

"All tired out," Abel said, yawning again. "Feel all let down—kind of satisfied and filled up inside my mind, like I'd had a big dinner—"

Mrs. Frake put her sewing down. "You and I are

going out right now and see what this Fair is all
about! All you've seen of it is the Swine Pavilion—"

"All you've seen of it is dirty dishes," Abel replied, yawning for the third time.

"It's the Fair! Come on, now."

Abel looked up with an expression of lazy anticipation which made Melissa think of him always
as a child, as she had thought of him when he was
her young lover. He pretended to attempt to rise
from the chair and to sink back helplessly.

"I guess this needle will get you out of there!"

"Melissa! Don't you dare—" She continued to
advance upon him with a bloodthirsty—or at least,
her notion of a bloodthirsty—expression upon her
face. "Melissa, if you touch me with that needle
I'll—"

"Then you get up!" Melissa said, fiercely. "You
used to be glad enough to get to take me on merry-
go-rounds and things."

"Oh, Lord," Abel said. "Merry-go-rounds!"

He rose with affected effort. "I'll take you down
and buy your ticket, but you can't get me on one
of those little horses."

Melissa gurgled. "You'll ride a little horse, too. A

big man like you, afraid of a little horse! You
ought to be ashamed. Fix your suspenders! And put
on your coat."

Abel put his suspenders back over his shoulders
and went into the tent for his coat. As he returned
to Melissa he sighed heavily, but she looked into his
eyes, studiously drawn in lines of care, and she
giggled.

An hour later Melissa stepped off the roller
coaster. "Heavens!" she remarked.

"Margy's crazy about it," Abel told her. He
had caught his breath.

A far-away look came into Melissa's eyes.
"There's a thing that swings around a lot of little
airplanes—I don't think it's so far from here."

Abel stopped. "All right. What is there after
that?"

Melissa looked up at him with eyes pleading and
confident.

"Cotton candy," she said.

"You can put that stuff on your face if you want
to. You're just a pickler. I'm a hogger, I've got to
remember my dignity."

"All right, Hogger. I see the swing!"

And another hour later they were climbing back

up the hill. "I ought to be spanked and spanked right," Melissa said, a little dolefully. "It's time to start supper and I haven't done a thing on the mending. We're going to get back to Brunswick all ragged and tattered."

"All right if we do. *You've seen the Fair!*" He paused for a moment as they separated before the two tents. He touched her arm with a caress that was almost timid.

Brazenly, she patted his hand.

Margy rose from dinner that evening, after an endless day, and announced that she was going to clean up the dishes and then disappear and see the Fair. Mrs. Frake also rose, and between them the two women had the table cleared in a few moments. Abel drifted toward a tent in which lived a farmer from Wapello, a stanch, conservative, anti-Brookhart Republican. A few seconds later they were quoting incorrect statistics at each other and rebutting with figures equally inaccurate.

Margy picked up her hat. "I think I'll run over to the Exhibition Hall and watch them beginning to tear out the exhibits."

"Well, Margy," her mother said, "I don't see how you can get any pleasure out of a sight like that, but if you can, go ahead. Only try not to stay out *all* night."

Margy kissed her mother and laughed. "Mother, why you should worry I don't know. Every evening when I come home, ever so early, you and Father are always sound asleep. But I'll come home pretty soon."

She went into her cubicle of the tent, changed her clothes, made up her face with great care and came quietly out. Abel had hinted at dark-beery secrets of his past and was strolling down toward the Midway to have a drink of near-beer with the conservative Republican whose tent was next door. They were using the smooth, quiet gesticulations of their most heated argument. They were settling Brookhart—Smith Brookhart, for some time an Iowa Senator.

Her mother was sitting with two neighbor ladies on a bench under the trees. All three were mending.

Margy slipped away quietly, hurried across the little wooden bridge over the gully, and went toward the roller-coaster. The third night, the last night, and the fourth night since she had met him. She tore into her heart and tried to find shame and penitence; she found only ecstasy and an anticipation which shimmered like thin flame from her thighs to her armpits. He had been so gentle, and so sure with her, perfectly aware that her desire was at least equal to his own, and yet he knew that she was not a loose woman—he knew that he was the first.

And what would he do to-night? If he passed her off with some halting and transparent pretense that they should meet again, then she would despise him and try to forget him—could she forget him? She went on, with expectancy and fear showing her the way.

Some one caught her arm as she started to mount the steps to the little latticed platform of the roller-coaster where she always waited for Pat. She turned abruptly. He held his hat in his hand. She had never seen him put the light Panama on his head. His extraordinary hair and his keen, joyous face were somehow enveloped in a nimbus, which because it was familiar was so much the more extraordinary.

"You're early," and his eyes read her face eagerly.

"You're early, too."

"Yes," he squeezed her hand. "I'm early, too. I thought you might want to come early—and if you didn't, still I didn't want to miss the chance to have another minute with you. To-night's the last night."

"Yes," she said, vaguely, "to-night's the last night of the Fair—the last night that really counts."

They got into the little car of the roller-coaster and it began to move slowly forward. He put his arm about her shoulders as they started up the first, long, incredibly vertical ascent.

"Do you know," she said, "I'm still afraid of this first drop, but now I like to be afraid. I'm afraid of the curve, too, but I always look forward to it, because there you hold me—closer—"

They shot down the slope which, being slightly less than perpendicular, hardly merited the name of slope, and around the quivering curve. The second drop fell under them and they came out into a series of waving turns and straightaways.

"I thought that first time that I'd be killed sure, and I didn't want to die, but I shouldn't mind it half so much, with you holding me, and with what I've had from it all since that night."

"You're splendid," he said, and his voice trembled. "I told you that night that you were the bravest thing I'd ever known. To-night I don't know how to tell you how wonderful you are. You take

206

life and brave it, and enjoy it. And you're beautiful, gallant—"

She stopped him with a pressure of her hand as the car drew in to the landing. They sat still and he showed his press card.

"Frakes," she said quietly, as they drew up that long ascent which gave them a moment's silence again, "think you ought to manage things and not let things manage you. I'll bet if Job turned up in the Frake family with God's hand against him, that when he scattered ashes on his head he'd pick out ashes that were good for the hair."

He shook with amusement, even as they were swooping down that long plunge. And then as they started around the vicious curve, when the car trembled and rose and fell upon the tracks, he said so close to her ear that she could hear, "—but it *would* be nice to die with you—" and as they straightened out toward the waves—"but nicer to live."

"Without me?"

"With you—"

She moved away from his arm. He stared at her, puzzled and hurt. "Things that seem best aren't always best, Pat." She looked at him with a quick, concealed wistfulness. The corners of his mouth quivered and he raised his eyebrows.

"I think a number of people have observed that, but why—?"

She ignored this and gazed at him with a seriousness which gave a kind of significance to the thing she said. "I'm afraid. I'm not afraid of things that will hurt me that I know will quit hurting. I'm afraid of things that might not ever quit."

"My God!" he said, with an assumption of ease, and he chanted, to a tune unfamiliar to her, an old satire on the platitude:

> *"Tho' to catch your drift I'm striving*
> *It is shady, it is shady,*
> *I don't see at what you're driving,*
> *Pretty lady, pretty lady."*

Then as he observed that she was totally unfamiliar with the works of W. S. Gilbert he added, "But why did you move away from me?"

She sighed. "I caught my elbow—I just moved."

He grasped her arm and moved it slowly upon the joint. "It works all right," he advised her, gravely, "now that I've fixed that—"

"Do you want to ride again?"

"No," he said, and looked at her eagerly. "By

God, you're the most beautiful, the most alive thing I've ever seen."

"Yes," she said, as if she had surrendered in an argument.

They stepped out of the car and he glanced at his wrist-watch. "It's still early. Is there anything you want to do?"

"Oh, let's run around as if we'd never seen a Fair before, and look at the exhibits and everything. I've never seen your exhibit from the Register—somebody said there were printing-machines of some kind—"

"Linotypes." He seemed uncomfortable. After a long time he said, "I'd love for you to see them, but you see most of the boys there know me—"

A cold and bitter chill struck her heart. "Oh— and you don't want them to see you with me—a country girl—?"

"Margy!" He grasped her arm angrily. "I'd rather they'd see me with you than anybody in the world. But before we go there you must promise me one thing."

"What?"

"That to-morrow—to-night—I can rake up the county clerk—you'll marry me."

Her heart and all her body sang, but she answered
calmly, "What's that got to do with it?"

He was definitely unhappy. "You've got me in
the devil of a hole. The fact is, Margy, I haven't
lived like a saint—hell, that's a stupid expression!
The fact is that I've been running around—a good
deal—and, of course, some of the women weren't
all they should be in any sense of the word—and
they've kissed and then told and those things get
around, through the girl's dearest friends, of course,
and—well, anyway when they see me with a girl
they think that I don't mean her any good, of
course."

She paused a long time to phrase the next inquiry
as she thought he would have phrased it. "Of course
your intentions toward me are and always have
been the same as my Sunday-school teacher's!"

"Damn it all, you can be difficult, too!" He
glanced at her with depression but not ill-humor.
"I never knew it to fail!" Then he was suddenly
serious. "Margy—please try to be decent—no, I
don't mean decent, I mean something more than
decent—please try to be masculine for a moment,
but only for a moment. I've asked you to promise
to marry me, because I love you. If I take you down

there and they see you with me, they'll remember
you and if they ever see you again under any circumstances—and a long life will turn up a lot of
circumstances—they'll say in a certain way, 'Oh,
yes, the first I saw that woman was with Pat Gilbert.' If you'll marry me, I don't care what they say
and neither do you. But if, by any chance, I'm going to have to follow you to your home and woo
you, maybe for a period of years, I don't want that
sort of talk going on—"

"Your life hasn't been—very—dull, has it, Pat?"

"No," he said doggedly, "it hasn't."

He waited a long time. "Do you want to go down
there?"

"I don't believe so, Pat."

He gave her a startled look. There was a silence,
an interminable silence, it seemed to her.

At last he spoke, with slightly forced cheerful-
ness. "Do you want to go outside the grounds with
me, a little way? Have you ever seen much of Des
Moines? It's nice, at night."

She looked at him with bitter humor, but he was
staring at his hands. "Thank you, I'd love to." She
bit her lip. It had sounded more ironic than she had
intended.

He made no sign of noticing. "How soon do you have to get home? It's about eight o'clock."

This time she answered naturally. "Oh, we needn't worry about that—or anything. The way the folks sleep these nights, if I get in any time before six it'll be all right.—I hope we'll be back before then?" It was shamelessly provocative, out of place, too, perhaps, just at this juncture. But the wild blood was racing through her temples.

He looked at her keenly. "We may not. I've got a lot—to say to you—this last night."

They found a taxi and rolled through the gates. He put his arms around her. It was all right, she thought. There wasn't going to be any quarrel, any breach between them, to-night. He even pointed out to her in his chaffing, friendly way, the points of interest that they passed, the talcum powder and lipstick factory, the patent medicine foundry on which rested the topmost branch of Des Moines aristocracy, the Greek Parthenon which was the police headquarters.

Margy looked at the great arches which stretched before them across the river. "It's only a small river here," she said. "At Brunswick, it's big, mysterious—"

Friday Evening: Margy

"In Brunswick," he said, very quietly, "every-thing is big and mysterious. I never realized it be-fore." He looked down at her thoughtfully. "I thought it was all Main Street from here to Dubuque —that's a nice town—but I've never really known before a person who associated with rivers on terms of equality."

She studied his face, decided that it was not a gibe.

"But you seem to hate all these people and things—"

"I wouldn't hate Brunswick," he assured her.

She laughed. "You remind me of the Storekeeper. He's a terribly nice person, too. But if you listened to him you'd think everything in the world was wrong."

She was surprised by the rebellious misery in his answer. "I think—my God!—I never really thought so, but now, I think—it is."

She was dumb with frightened conjecture. But in a moment he caught her up fiercely to him and be-gan to kiss her. There was, for several minutes, nothing but that.

Pat raised his head. The car had been speeding westward with them. They drove along a wide street for a way and suddenly he tapped on the window at the driver. The driver turned. He uttered a number. Margy looked at him questioningly.

"Just a friend's place," he said.

"But I'm not dressed to meet people—" It was a feeble subterfuge.

The cab swung in to the curb and stopped. He paid the driver, took her arm and led her into the foyer of a building before he answered. "You won't."

A long time afterward she said quietly. "Let's go now. Let's go back to the grounds."

He looked at her, his eyes shining. He shook his graceful shoulders as an Atlas might, having felt the world roll off. "No, Margy. Not for a moment. Not until you'll promise me that we are going to the county clerk's office to-morrow morning and that we'll be married to-morrow afternoon."

She looked at him without answering. She was not thinking of his words, but only looking at him, warm, carefree, boyish in her arms.

"Margy," he said. "To-morrow, I tell you. You shall have lilies of the valley, even if there isn't time for a veil."

Friday Evening: Margy

She moved her head slightly, just enough so that
he should not see the conflict of fear and longing in
her eyes. He sat up and looked at her, puzzled. "Pat
—let's not rush things. There are a lot of things to
think about."

"Rot," he said. "We know everything we need to
know, right now. . . . Don't be a little goose,
Margy. Or is it—the women I told you about a
while ago? Surely, Margy, darling—"

She laughed gently. "It would be pretty silly if
I wouldn't marry you because other women had
done what I've done, wouldn't it? No, I don't think
that that's it. I suppose that's an awful thing to say,
but I don't think it amounts to much—it's past."
She stopped. She had not much courage for what
she had to say.

"Then what on earth, Margy?" He was looking
a little hurt, on his dignity.

"Pat, have you thought that if you marry me
you'll tie yourself to one place, that you don't like,
and one woman, all your life? I wouldn't stand for
other women. It's not reasonable, it's just my
pride."

"Yes. I don't want anything or any one else. If I
can't manage myself," he grinned, "like a Frake,

215

then there's no use my fooling myself. I know that I'll hate the place—any place, for long, and that I'll see other women I'll want, but I'll want you, Margy, and want to keep you worse than anything. If I can't live in a way to keep you, I'm worse than I think I am."

"No more adventures? No more travels? Just slaving on your paper—you say you slave on it—until you're old?"

"Yes. I can do that—I hope. Of course, things might happen. Things really would happen." He was speaking more eagerly now. His eagerness strangely made her shiver. "We could go to Chicago, or New York."

"New York," said Margy. "How would I get along in New York? What would people think of me? I don't know any of the things they know."

"They'd think you were the most lovely creature who ever alighted on Manhattan. Fresh, sweet—the men would make love to you and the women would hate you." Then, after a pause, "Besides, those things you could learn—easily."

The first sentences had welled up out of his own tenderness. The last sounded—soberer.

She forged ahead. "What would your friends in

New York talk to me about? Back in Brunswick, I'd be useful and people would like me. I could run a house. I'd have children, four or five, and they'd grow up like me and live to bring more land into the family. We still like land, we farmers, even though it's nearly ruined us lately."

He was looking narrowly at her. "Whose children? Into whose family would this land be brought?"

His face frightened her, but she answered levelly. "Pat, it's hard to tell you—but—there is some one back home. He's been in love with me always, all my life. I'd be—"

He seized her wrist. "Margy! Are you telling me you love this—farmer back home? Are you trying to say that—"

The shock and outrage in his eyes she could not bear.

She clung to him. "Oh, no, Pat. No. It's just he loves me." Her honesty impelled her further. "And I love—his kind of life. I'd be—somebody—back there. And he'd always love me. You'll get bored with me after a while."

He caught her, kissed her almost cruelly. But the cloud in his eyes had not lightened. She knew, under

217

his kiss, that she had not been waging honest war-
fare. She had been setting up straw men of arguments for the joy of seeing him knock them down.
Had he knocked them down? She did not know.
She could fight no longer, for her strength had left
her.

He smoothed his hair, reached for his hat. "I'd
better be taking you back. Under the circumstances
—we don't want any trouble."

She followed him out and stood silent on the sidewalk while he called a taxicab. They rode to the
bridge without saying a word. She reached out and
put her hand on his arm. "Pat, don't hate me."

But the cab was drawing up at the entrance to
the Fair Grounds. A gatekeeper came forward to
see Pat's pass.

They walked together in silence through the
streets of the Fair. She saw that he was leading her
toward the bridge across the little ravine near
Campers' Hill. In the shadows under the trees he
put an arm around her waist and drew her down on
the grass beside him.

Afterward they lay looking at the stars through
the trees, his arm beneath her body, and hers beneath his neck. Hands clasped across their bodies,

they could feel the beating of each other's hearts.
They felt only a drowsy pleasure in their nearness
and the end of strife. Far off, down the hill, they
could hear the faint pounding of hammers, where
men were preparing to move the trappings of this
fair to other fairs.

"Margy," said Pat, "if it weren't to be—a happy
ending, I should feel now that they were—tearing
me down, too."

Her fingers moved against his face. She could not
speak.

At last it could not be put off. She must go to her
father's tent. But Pat held her by the hand, even
when she was ready to go. "To-morrow, Margy?"

She caught her breath. Then she answered, "Not
to-morrow, Pat. We're going home. I'll write you—
soon, Pat."

And she added, "How can I tell up here—so
soon? I love you, Pat, but sometimes you seem like
something—I'll wake up from. But I'll write—It's
so strange—if it had been back home—"

He nodded. "Soon, Margy." He kissed her. His
hair shone in the moonlight over the sleeping camp;
the hat tossed against his knee and he stooped, a
little, as always, as if he were pursuing some elusive

219

manifestation of God which he hoped suddenly to overtake, as he walked up the little rise on the other side of the ravine.

Strangely enough, this was the way she always remembered him.

FRIDAY EVENING: WAYNE

CHAPTER XII

FRIDAY EVENING: WAYNE

THE morning was endless. It was at two o'clock that life began, when he found her at the entrance of the field and said, "Come on, let's hurry, I'm late. The first race is already about to start and I've got my best bet on it."

Then she looked at him with a tenderness which took all the coldness from her words. She pressed his hand secretly.

"Did you get home all right?"

"Yes. I told them I'd just come from the bathhouse. You see, there's a place below the camp grounds where we all have to go to bathe and shave. I got a shave at a barber shop, but I had to tell him to leave the powder off, because I never use anything but witch hazel."

She laughed as they found places in the little inclosure. "How do you manage to remember things like that? I'd be caught a dozen times a day if I had to remember little things like powder—"

He shook his head. "I'm not a good enough liar to be able to afford to forget things like that. I don't know what I do, but the folks always spot me the first thing, if they're the least bit suspicious. Only, they haven't been suspicious about us."

"Wait a minute." She rushed over to the book-maker and came back with her slips. "I saw Dad to-day. He lost his socks the first day, because he thought these races were crooked like all the others. He told me the horses that ought to win, to lose my money on, and then he bet on the others. He didn't realize that farmers, some of them with race-horses of their own, would know a bad race in a minute and that they have to keep them right."

He seemed puzzled. "But how could they cheat?"

She laughed. "You're such an innocent. They beat their horses with the whip and hold them back with the bridle—a little twist."

"But you could see by how the horse held its head—"

"*You* could, and all of these farmers could—every move the horse made would mean something to you—but the ordinary crowd of touts and gamblers couldn't. They study their horses on paper —they know what it has done and they can tell by

watching it how it can run, but they can't tell what
the horse thinks by watching its gestures."

"And you mean there are lots of crooked race-
tracks?"

"All of them but two. This one is all right, and I
suppose there must be another one somewhere. I've
only been to forty or fifty. Anyway, after the first
day, Dad made so much money he couldn't spend
it all on liquor and—entertainment—" She glanced
at him, caught his thought and said defensively,
"He may raise the devil, but he's done everything
he had any notion should be done for me. And he's
bought a nice farm, down in Missouri, that we can
fix up and pretend is our home, if we ever wanted
to go to it."

The horses lined up. There was a shot and they
galloped down the track, then wheeled and stopped.
The barrier was still up. Again the performance was
repeated, the barrier rose, and they swung around
the curve of the first furlong. Instinctively, Wayne
caught Emily by the elbows and lifted her above the
heads about them.

The race went its way, she collected what was
due her, placed her bets and returned to him. "I lost
four dollars, net," she said. "Anyhow, I'm going

down there after the fairs are over and get things in shape and fix it up with some furniture. It's got a big fireplace and they say there's still some shooting around in the hills—wild turkeys and such stuff—and Dad's coming down. We'll probably have a cozy winter until he gets the bug again, about February, and goes down to outguess those burglars in Havana and Bermuda."

"It's in the Ozarks?"

"Yes. The house is right on top of a little mountain."

"It's no good for farming."

She glanced at him amusedly. "Neither is Fifth Avenue, but I could lie down and gasp my little soul out with joy if some one would give me forty acres along Fifth Avenue in a spot I'd pick."

He flushed. "You know what I meant. Your race is about to start."

She caught his hand again, lightly. "Of course I do. It's just a pleasure place. I don't suppose we'll be there four months a year."

The race ran through, and after it, many races. It was four thirty when they finally crowded through the field entrance and found themselves in the only moderate crowds of the Midway walk.

Friday Evening: Wayne

She casually led the way to the sidewalk café where they had first eaten together.

"Don't eat much," she warned. "I've won"—she consulted a little note-book—"one hundred and forty-four dollars on the races since the first day and to-night is my night to howl. We're going downtown and eat the best the city affords. Then we're going to see a show and then"—her voice trembled the least bit—"I am going to bid you a fond farewell."

"It all sounds fine to me but the last. I think," he said quietly, "we had better postpone the fond farewells for about a hundred years."

She sighed. "I wish we could. But Daddy's leaving to-morrow morning and your folks will be getting ready to go. Oh, well, let's eat and not think about it—this is my party—I've still got about fifty dollars left—and we're not going to think or talk about things we don't like until we have to."

He caught her hand under the table. "Maybe not now, but finally we're going to talk about such things, and I'm opposed to farewells—even fond ones—between you and me."

They ate then, almost in silence. Afterward they wandered down to the gate of the grounds and caught a taxicab. Like that other day, it was very warm. Men were wiping their foreheads with wet handkerchiefs at the street-car loading station; women looked distressed; children cursed nature in all the whining and bawling tones of childhood. But in their cab the fresh breeze of motion kept them cool—kept her so cool that she quickly regained a gay glitter, a sheen on her personality, which he had never been able to analyze.

They drove across the Northwestern tracks, down past the powder manufactory, and came through quiet streets, lined with trees, to the State Historical Building.

"That's nice," said Wayne. "That looks cool and pleasant. I want you to see something that's in there."

They left the taxicab and walked up the marble steps, Emily wondering somewhat. Magnificent Ionic pillars ushered them into the high cool entrance hall. Ahead there were steps with a stained-glass window behind them and they went up to the second floor.

"Only ten minutes left," a guard said, warningly.

Wayne guided Emily. They came out in a tiny

gallery of pictures and he led her to one which showed a white-haired man, a little reminiscent of Andrew Jackson in his less demagogic moods, but stern and sure, sitting quietly and smiling at the man who had painted—or drawn, originally—his picture.

"My great-grandfather," Wayne said simply.

She studied the picture for a long time. A gong sounded through the building, and they hurried out between groups of buffalo, deer, and wolves to the entrance.

"It wasn't worth while after all," Wayne said.

She drew a long breath—sighed. "It was worth while," she said, rather strangely.

Finally a taxicab came, and they started on toward the bridge which connected East and West Des Moines. "Everything must have been much easier in those days," she said. "He believed everything that was printed in books, and knew exactly what was right and what was wrong, and all he ever needed to know about any woman he fell in love with was whether she'd have plenty of children. If he couldn't marry her, then he could marry another one, just as good."

Wayne sat up, indignantly. "My great-grandfather married a girl back in Ohio that the doctors said would die in a year of consumption; he married the girl because he loved her, and he waited a year to come to Iowa, until she died. It was twenty-five years before he married the next time."

"I'm sorry, Wayne. Of course they must have been pretty much like us. I say things—a little bit reckless, sometimes."

"Oh, no," he said placidly enough. "Lots of people who never lived on farms have the same kind of an idea—that with women we're just a lot of animals like our hogs and horses—"

She caught his arm and drew it to her side, against her breast, intimately. "Wayne! Of course I know you're not like that—and you know I know it! Please forgive me."

He kissed her quickly, glancing through the windows of the cab to see that he was not observed. "I know what you meant, Emily. It wasn't the place —it was the time. They wanted lots of children in those days because the time needed people, there were lots of places to settle, lots of new things to do—it was all a kind of excitement—like after a war—like now."

She nodded. The taxicab was crossing the river

and in a few moments it slid by the public library, ran up ten blocks or so of Locust Street and stopped before her hotel. Wayne tossed the taxicab driver a bill—it was his last ten dollars—took his change and followed Emily into the hotel. They went straight to the elevator and her room.

"You'll want to wash here, and comb your hair," she said, "but we'll go somewhere else for dinner. It's just possible that Dad might decide to eat here. I'll get into my dinner dress."

When he emerged from the bathroom she had slipped into the lacy garment in which he had seen her on the first of those nights together. He caught her about the waist and turned her face up to his. "I still can't believe that anything so wonderful could have happened to *me!*"

She gave him her warm, intimate laugh, and held his face while he kissed her. "That can wait," she said. "Now we've got to go to dinner."

He followed her with a little sense of discontent. Somehow, when he meant to talk seriously to her, she evaded him. Next it was the crowded dining-room of another hotel, with very large napkins and more silver than two men would need to eat three meals. The lights were dim in their corner and the waiter, though attentive, paused always a safe distance out of earshot. But somehow he could not talk to her seriously while he was eating. It seemed undignified.

At last it was all over. She lighted a cigarette and gave one to him, from a tiny enameled case. "I'll smoke one," he said, "but they don't mean anything."

She laughed. "What do you mean by that?"

He wrinkled his nose. "They don't smell like anything, especially. I like the smoke from Dad's cigars, but these things, when they don't actually smell bad, don't smell like anything."

She blew out a mouthful of smoke and sniffed it critically. "It doesn't smell like much, does it? I guess it's just the kick you get from the nicotine. It's a habit."

He puffed twice more on his gently, and then put it in the ash-tray and affected to forget it. She giggled. "Wayne, you're the silliest fool I've ever seen—and the nicest." She inhaled a breath of smoke, blew it out and put out her cigarette.

"Do you really want to see a show much, Wayne?"

Friday Evening: Wayne

The blood leaped in his veins, so that even she could see the throb of blue at his temples, under the clear, browned skin.

"No, you don't," she said softly; "let's go up to the room."

He sat down in a chair near the window and she made him a drink—one of those drinks which he still considered the most sinful episodes in his life. He sipped it and looked at her thoughtfully. She sat down on the edge of the bed with her drink and slipped off her shoes, wriggling the toes of her small foot with evident relief. She looked across at him and her face became thoughtful and unhappy— wistful.

"What's the matter, Emily?"

"This is the last evening, Wayne."

"Don't believe it. There'll be lots more evenings all our lives. You don't think I'm going to let you slip away from me now?"

The liquor gave him a sense of power, a certainty of well-being.

She shook her head, smiled, and again he had the sense that she had evaded him. Suddenly she rose from the bed, came close to him and caressed him as he gave her a long embrace. He picked her up in his strong arms and carried her to the bed. They sat down there together, like two children.

"Emily, why have you been so far away from me this evening? I want to take you over to the folks to-morrow and tell them we're going to get married. To-night, you act as if we weren't—you act as if I'd done something. What have I done? This is the last night; you can't afford to keep anything from me now, because if we quarreled now, we'd never see each other again."

She was about to reply, then thought better of it and stopped his questions with her mouth. Usually she could make him forget everything, but to-night he was pertinacious. He held her close, but finally he released her.

"You must love me—if I didn't think you loved me I'd never want to see you again, and I'd be sick of myself."

"I do love you, Wayne, but we'll never see each other again."

He was perplexed and, being a man, his perplexity was part annoyance. "But we must see each other again! Really, we're married. Really, you're

234

my wife. I've taken that for granted since—What do you mean?"

She smiled gently and shook her head. "I'm terribly sorry, Wayne. If I'd loved you when I first saw you as I do now, if I'd known how true and sweet—and—naïve—you are, I'd never have brought us—you and me—to this. I do love you, but I wouldn't marry you for anything in the world."

He was shocked. "But why—" Suddenly he burst out in anger. "For God's sake, Emily, quit all this mysterious stuff and tell me what you're thinking of." His anger became bitter. "I don't know how it is among the people you know, but among people back on the farm, when a girl's been to a man what you've been to me, it's generally supposed that she'll marry him—that she has, really, married him."

For one moment her eyes were angry. "What have I been to you? I've loved you because you were fine and sweet, and because you deserved it—then. I doubt even that you know much of the habits of 'people of your kind' in those matters, when you talk like that, but can't you see that it's impossible for us to marry—if I hadn't thought you'd know that—"

At his look of bewilderment her tone became gentler. She patted his hand. "Can you imagine me living on your farm, Wayne, milking cows and all that sort of thing—?"

"The Hired Man milks the cows," he interrupted stiffly.

"I don't know anything about farms," she said, impatiently, "except that what you would expect of your wife is something I couldn't be—how can you be so silly?" She was near crying.

"Emily, dear," he said, "you could live any way you wanted to. We'd have enough money so you wouldn't have to do anything you didn't want to. You could go over to Fairfield or to Farmview or Ottumwa any time you felt like it. They're not great big towns, but they have shows and that sort of thing. There's not even much to manage. You could have a hired girl that would do everything for you."

"And how would you like me if I married you on just those terms?"

"I'd stick to anything I've said—"

"I know you would. That wasn't what I asked. I

asked what you would think of me. And if I didn't want to have any babies what would become of your precious Frakes?" She giggled hysterically. "Do I look like a 'farm girl,' Wayne? It's simply impossible."

"You didn't love me at all?"

She looked at him despairingly. "Of course I did and do. The thought of any other man, it makes me sick—now. But can't you see that even though we could marry and be happy, our lives can't marry and be happy?" She put her hand gently on his leg. "What idiots men are! The first time I ever saw you, I wanted you. I wouldn't have lived my life out without you and remembering you for anything—it will probably be a beastly life, as far as that goes. And the first time I ever saw you I knew I'd rather die than marry you. . . . Now you'll always be something sweet—wonderful—to me. And I hope I will be to you. If we married it would just be one battle after another. If I were the kind of woman you want to marry we'd never have met in the first place—certainly we'd never have had this week."

He rose slowly. "I suppose I ought to be getting back to the tent."

She rose, too, and stood by the desk in the corner. Her dress somehow gave her the effect of slenderness, though she was sumptuous, generous. She looked at him with a strange smile. He pulled on his coat.

"Wayne, you know perfectly well that I'm right. Hasn't this—all—been pleasant for you? Why should you try to make something more of it than there is in it? You came up to a State Fair, you found a—girl—who—at least, did you no harm. Can't you let it go at that?"

Striding toward the door with fury in his face, he stopped suddenly. Then he turned and came slowly back. "You're right, of course," he said quietly. "I knew you were right, but I didn't want to think so. I hate to think of it being all over. But I was raised to run a farm—and you weren't—and we couldn't ever reach middle ground. Only, I love you!"

"My dear—Wayne, dear heart—" She ran toward him and then halted herself. "Oh, Wayne, I didn't mean it to come to this. You're beautiful and I'm not ugly, and I thought—no one cares if there's a little more pleasure in the world. And besides, I liked you for other things—I liked you even because you were so proud and devoted to your family, and because you were strong, and because you were so sure that everything always comes out right if you just manage it, and I loved you because you have a little birthmark on your forehead, just where the hair ends, and because the vein in your temple always throbs—when you love me—most—but I can't cheat us both, my dearest, I can't marry you—"

He stepped across the thin, infinite border between boyhood and manhood. "I'll never know any one I love as much as you—but I'll be happier with —another woman." His hands cupped themselves about her body. "We still have to-night—"

END OF A KERMESS

CHAPTER XIII

END OF A KERMESS

"ARE you all ready?" Abel asked, sitting above the wheel, the gears, and the levers of the truck, a kind of Destiny poised over what had been Fair Week.

"Everything's in," said Mrs. Frake, and she sighed. "There's not near as much as when we started. We've picked up quite a lot of stuff, but we've eaten more than that, and with glass that was broken and packing we didn't need, it comes out a lot lighter than when we left home."

Momentarily their minds flashed back to that evening, with the red sunset colors on the sky, and they looked toward the west. The sky was still red and the few horizon clouds came up in purples and slate blues.

"A hundred and twenty-five miles," said Abel. "I'm glad I got me a good rest last night. Though we can drive considerably faster and if Blue Boy doesn't like it, he can lump it. He isn't a prima donna any more. I can't figure how such a hog with a disposition like he's got, got so famous all of a sudden."

Margy, hidden between her father's shoulder and her mother's, smiled secretly, and then she did not smile.

"My goodness, Margy," said Mrs. Frake, "what's the matter with you? Here you're crying as if there wasn't ever going to be any more State Fairs. We'll all be up here again next year, and a year isn't much —not after you've lived a lot of them."

Margy did not respond.

"What's the matter with you back there, Wayne? My goodness, you don't seem to me like the same youngsters came up to the Fair with me."

The truck groaned crazily up the gully and Margy turned to give a glance to a forgotten alcove in the trees—a moment later Wayne saw the place where the booth of the hoop-la man had been. They passed the truck of the neighbor from Wapello County and saw that the family was still loading.

Abel waved gaily. "Hope you get out, all right. See you next year! Down with Dan Steck, the broad-striped Whatisit! Hooray for Brookhart! See you next year, old man."

End of a Kermess

From the bath-house they heard the pouring of showers—concession men who had torn down their tents and were preparing for hot rides on freight cars to the next State Fair. There were shouts and laughing.

It was just lighting time for the grounds and a few dismal bulbs threw uncertain glares at street corners, but there were great pools of gray dusk where all the sparkle of the other nights had been. The truck hit a line of bumps where the paving had been torn up, just at the end of the Fair Grounds. There was an asphalting machine, sulphurous and hot, and a steam-roller, held in doubtful restraint until the truck passed by. Blue Boy cursed the paving gang with bitter and filthy curses and they answered him with delighted squeals. There was no overtone in their voices to indicate that they knew their ancestors were being muddied by the greatest hog who had ever lived and bred.

The truck turned after it had left the Grounds and passed along the side of the Swine Pavilion toward the open road. Blue Boy raised his snout and snuffed at the cool evening air. His eyes were still capable of some little expression and at this time they showed what a keen and practised observer might have recognized as bewilderment—not pleased bewilderment.

He whooshed twice, perhaps with doubt, perhaps with passion, but the progress of the truck took the Swine Pavilion beyond his convenient range of vision—he lay down. He sniffed; he dozed.

Mrs. Frake turned to her daughter.

"Margy, get hold of yourself. You're too old to do things like this! This isn't going to be the last State Fair in the world."

"I wish it were," said Margy.

Mrs. Frake patted her daughter's arm. "You're just at an age when everything seems twice as important as it really is. Now don't worry, baby, because next year we'll be back up here again—unless you're up here with your own family. I wouldn't be surprised—"

"By George, you know," said Abel Frake, "I wouldn't have believed if you'd told me a week ago that I was going to drive home with a trophy, and a plaque, and so on, that I could've felt so kind of melancholy as I do to-night. They might leave the lights on the grounds till we get out, anyway."

He directed the truck expertly but swiftly, and

when Blue Boy complained he was answered with a patronizing cluck. "Of course, you don't like it, but it's time for you to realize that you're not the big stuff in this family. Another year or two, you'll be making bacon. Of course, your skin's going to be mounted in the State Historical Building, right along with pictures of my own people, but folks ain't going to admire it for the same reasons."

Blue Boy told him that his ancestors were of no particular interest to the proud family of the swine, which stretched back into antiquity to a time when no one had heard of Frakes.

"Oh, shut up, you silly, grunting, squeaking fool," said Wayne.

Blue Boy paused for a moment. Then he spoke at slow, grunting length; his characterizations of Wayne were cynical, but his surmises were exact.

"Listen!" said Wayne, "if you don't shut off that racket I'm going to give you a good kick in the slats. I want some peace and quiet."

Blue Boy snuffled, complacently. Then he went to sleep. Wayne growled at him. The truck ran past the last houses of Des Moines on the road to Prairie City. Twilight was dropping rapidly and already a periodic blaze of light swept over the car

247

and retreated in a great arc. "The air-mail beacon," Abel said, after it had done this the fifth or sixth time.

Margy stopped crying and peered out at the sides of the road. They saw lights turned on in some of the houses, lights with humanity behind them. But Margy did not wonder what life was behind the lights; she did not feel the little *Weltschmerz* which she had suffered on the trip from home—she wondered what Pat was doing. She starved for him. He had said, "I believe everything in the world is wrong."

"You children are certainly keeping mighty quiet," Mrs. Frake observed. "Now come on and liven up—we're going to have supper pretty soon before it gets real dark, and then you'll feel better."

The car drove around the square at Prairie City and set out for Pella. Now and again other cars coming from the Fair passed the truck and most of the drivers shouted pleasantries about the hog, to which Abel replied good-naturedly. Occasionally a "dirt farmer" recognized the animal and yelled his congratulations to Abel over the noise of the motors.

A little out of Prairie City they stopped the car

beside a green slope and Melissa spread the picnic cloth. Abel turned the lights of the car so that "we can see what kind of bugs we're eating" and they sat down to thick slices of cold roast ham, chicken wings, pickled beets, onion rings in sweet pickle, cold cherry pie, and iced tea. In spite of themselves Wayne and Margy felt more cheerful when they climbed back into the truck. It was dark now, but the road was alight with cars and they soon passed through Pella where the Dutch farmers were enjoying their Saturday evening in town boisterously, like good peasants.

"Making good time," said Abel, "at this rate we'll be home by midnight and all get a good night's sleep."

"That's fine," said Melissa, who had been fighting an overpowering drowsiness ever since they had eaten. "I can hardly keep my eyes open. I don't know how I got so tired."

Abel laughed and patted her hand. "I know how you got so tired, Mama. You've just finished your hardest week's work of the year."

Melissa opened her eyes about one third, smiled and shook her head. "Had a lot of fun. State Fair is worth waiting for the whole year." She slept.

"What are you doing back there, son?"

There was no answer. Wayne was industriously engaged in attempting to outsnore Blue Boy. Added to emotional overstrain, nights which had not been exactly restful, and the usual excitement of Fair Week, the supper had hit him like ether.

Abel turned to Margy with a grin. "Well, honey, I hope you'll try to stay awake and keep me company." He looked at her more closely. "What's the matter, baby, aren't you feeling good?"

"I think—the—the food and the water—and everything—are upsetting me—my stomach—feels funny—"

"I wouldn't be a bit surprised. Do you want me to stop a minute and let you walk around a little? Maybe the truck's making you seasick."

She struggled for a moment. "No, Daddy, I'll be all right, I guess."

He drove a little way in silence. "You just speak up if you want to stop." There was another silence. Then, talking more to himself than to her, he added, "All this excitement might upset anybody—not but what women's stomachs are funny. . . . We're going to be pulling into Oskaloosa around ten. Maybe we could stop there and get you some hot coffee or some aspirin." Abel had always been so solicitous about his children's aches and illnesses that they had never, before their teens, minded a little attack of measles or mumps. The cash value of the disease exceeded its distresses.

"We'll see how I feel when we get there, Daddy. It's kind of going off now, I think."

Abel looked at her fondly. "I suppose that when you're a grown woman with ten kids I won't be able to realize that Melissa doesn't have to wash your face and paddle your pants. I can see that you and Wayne are bigger, but darned if you ever seem changed to me."

"What makes you say that?"

"Oh, I know, kids have their little troubles, too, that seem pretty important to them. I'd bet a dollar, just from the way you acted, that you had a fight with Harry just before we left."

She pouted, "Oh, we're always fighting."

He laughed contentedly. "That's good. Hope you form a lifelong habit. Harry's a good sound boy, and smart. There's no danger the Chicago Land Bank'll ever get that place."

"I can't imagine what you're talking about!"

"Oh, I knew you wouldn't. I'm just wandering

on in my doddering way. You go ahead and catch
some sleep, Margy."

"I'm not sleepy."

"Feeling better?"

"Lots better." The truck ran on. When it reached
Oskaloosa, whose streets were still thronged, Margy
was sleeping against her father's shoulder.

Abel Frake smiled. By deliberately snapping off
his sense of direction he could almost imagine that
he was driving, as he had been driving seven days
before, to the carnival—to the Fair. There was
Blue Boy murmuring objections at every pit in the
road; there was the sleeping family; there was the
yellow roadway with its fringe of varying shadow;
there was the crackling mist of light which was
the universe, spread out over Abel Frake at regular
intervals, and over Blue Boy, the finest Hampshire
stud boar in the world.

That, of course, ended the illusion and with surprise Abel Frake realized that he was glad that he
was not going to the Fair—that he was going home.
He was gorged with the excitement and the
triumphs of that strange place; reality, as he had
made it for himself, pleased and satisfied him. The
Frakes had stepped for a moment into a fantasy;

now, unchanged, they were returning to that five hundred acres where only birth and death—not even marriage—had been the only changes for four generations.

The streets were quiet in Eddyville. The corner lights still glowed dutifully. The house that had been lighted was dark. He would never know what had happened there and he would never care. All this interval had been only the extinguishing of a lamp.

Margy stirred and turned her head on his shoulder. He moved her face gently so that she would be more comfortable. There was still a little bustle in Ottumwa and Melissa half-woke at the vibration of cobble stones.

"Almost home?"

"Almost—Ottumwa."

She patted his knee and returned to sleep.

Ottumwa went home from the movies and Abel drove on toward Eldon. After Eldon he would drive on the river road, down past Selma, Douds and Brunswick, beside waters which would lick at the edge of his farm hours later. He liked the river. It made him think of Indians, and the Church Tree—the great elm under which his grandfather had arranged the first religious services ever held in that part of Iowa—and of things so old and enduring that they did not even disquiet his mortality.

The tiny towns slid by darkly. The engine quivered up through the steering-wheel and gave Abel a curious sense of power.

He touched the accelerator with his toe. At his least signal they fled across the world more swiftly, more slowly, as he wished. Brunswick went by.

The Hired Man met them, full of excitement, questions and jubilation. Margy looked at the house, which had been open to air all day, stout and spreading and homely. Had she ever left here? Through her drowsiness she felt some memory that she was changed, but how she did not know. She felt, here in the yard at home, that there had been no Fair, no change, no Pat.

"You folks run on to bed," said Abel. "We'll put the prima donna away in his pen."

The Hired Man regarded the great hog friendlily. "You're a homely old devil," he said gleefully to Blue Boy, "but when better little piggies is made, they'll address you as 'Papa.' "

Blue Boy painfully opened one eye as he climbed

down the ramp to his pen. Mud! He could smell fresh mud. From the shadow of the overhang came two various grunts. Blue Boy slowly turned his head one inch toward the Hired Man. "Whoosh!" he said contemptuously. "Whoosh! Ungggh!"

"Absolutely," said the Hired Man. "You gointa put the trophy in there with him, Abel, or do we just bring it out for him to look at feeding times?"

Abel laughed. "Say, would you mind putting up the truck? I'm feelin' just a little mite sleepy myself."

EPILOGUE: THE STOREKEEPER

CHAPTER XIV

EPILOGUE: THE STOREKEEPER

SUNDAY dinner, in that country, meant a twelve-
o'clock meal followed by five hours of "visiting,"
then a picnic supper and two more hours of "visiting" until one of the guests said something vague
about bedtime.

So when the Storekeeper's ancient and cheap car
—he had always known that cars gave the Powers
an unfair advantage and never risked an extra nickel
on one—drew up in the Frake driveway, he was not
surprised to see on the front porch, Mr. and Mrs.
Frake, Harry, Margy, Wayne, Eleanor, and Eleanor's widowed father. The men were smoking
cigars, the women were eating Mrs. Frake's candy,
all had obviously supped recently and well.

Abel hastened out to greet the visitor. "Well,"
he said, "it's the Storekeeper!" His surprise seemed
sincere although the car had driven practically
across the porch in passing to the driveway, and
every one in the township knew the Storekeeper's

259

car not only by sight but by sound. "Come on up and have a piece of cake and some ice tea."

"Ice tea?"

"Eleanor and Wayne brought a chunk of ice over from Pittsville with them. There's still a little bit left."

"I was wondering," said the Storekeeper. "I knew the ice-house gave out before you went to the Fair."

"Bad harvest last winter. Mighty glad you came around. You don't go visiting much." Abel was apparently completely unconscious of the purpose of the Storekeeper's visit.

"Oh, I like to look in on people occasionally. Kind of keep in touch with my clientele. Sometimes it gives me some good ideas on how much credit to let them have."

The group on the porch hailed him. He returned the salutations and sat down on the edge of the raised porch.

The Storekeeper glanced at Margy and suddenly the corners of his eyes turned into three, shrewd, amiable wrinkles. And yet there was surprise in those small lines etched out in the brown face. She let her glance wander away, and the Storekeeper turned to Wayne.

Epilogue: The Storekeeper

"What do you think of Des Moines?"

"It's all right—too big."

For a moment a kind of astonishment showed on the Storekeeper's face. If Abel had noticed he would have remembered that the Storekeeper had been astonished in 1904, when the Big Flood took away all of the loose parts of Brunswick, but not since. But Abel did not notice.

"Nice breeze you've got here, right up from the river. My, the trees are certainly getting yellow, aren't they?"

"Well, you can't keep the year from getting along," Abel said, sententiously, watching the Storekeeper with suppressed amusement. "By the way, would you like to take a look at Blue Boy since he's won all his honors?"

"No," said the Storekeeper, "he'd probably make me cry."

"Cry," said Eleanor's father, blankly. "Why?"

"Why, how can you ask why?" asked the Storekeeper with astonishment. "Here's the proudest animal of a whole species, glutted with honors and cracked wheat, and all for what? Trophies to-day, ham to-morrow." He coughed significantly. "If you'd ask him to-night, I'll bet he'd say that everything that's happened to him has happened for the best. Little does he suspect that every ounce he puts on just encourages the butcher. There's people could take advantage of his example."

Eleanor's father laughed gustily. "You talk like a preacher. Man that is born of woman, or something of that sort."

"I do talk something like a preacher," the Storekeeper said mildly, "though I'm opposed to them as a class."

Wayne changed the subject hastily. His prospective father-in-law had the scrupulous religiosity of a man wholly illiterate religiously.

"How's business been?"

"Too good," said the Storekeeper. "I remember business in 1903 and 1910 and 1913 and 1920. I've let my stock get a way down. We're going to have a depression and a big one before another year's out." He looked at Abel. "You sell off your crops and your stock and don't buy anything till next winter. Business is too good. Whenever everybody spends a lot of money, then pretty soon they haven't got any money to spend."

Abel regarded him seriously, as did Wayne and Harry. "You think so? Times seem to promise to be